The Blue Shoe

ALSO BY RODERICK TOWNLEY

The Blue Shoe

A Tale of Thievery, Villainy, Sorcery, and Shoes

by Roderick Townley

illustrated by Mary GrandPré

ALFRED A. KNOPF

NEW YORK

THIS IS A BORZOI BOOK PUBLISHED BY ALFRED A. KNOPF

Visit us on the Web! www.randomhouse.com/kids
Educators and librarians, for a variety of teaching tools, visit us at
www.randomhouse.com/teachers

Library of Congress Cataloging-in-Publication Data
Townley, Rod.
The blue shoe : a tale of thievery, villainy, sorcery, and shoes / by Roderick Townley ;
illustrated by Mary GrandPré. — 1st ed.
  p. cm.
Summary: A mysterious stranger commissions a single, valuable shoe from a humble cobbler, changing the cobbler's life and the life of his young apprentice forever.
ISBN 978-0-375-85600-6 (trade) — ISBN 978-0-375-95600-3 (lib. bdg.) — ISBN 978-0-375-89417-6 (e-book)
[1. Fables.] I. GrandPré, Mary, ill. II. Title.
PZ8.2.T67Bl 2009
[Fic]—dc22
2008043851

The text of this book is set in 12-point Goudy.

Printed in the United States of America
October 2009
10 9 8 7 6 5 4 3 2
First Edition

For Wyatt—
hope it fits

Contents

PART ONE

Grel

One

Not long ago, in the sunny mountain village of Aplanap, famous for its tilted streets, cuckoo clocks, and Finster cheese, there stood a small shoemaker's shop. And in the window of that shop was a shoe that fit nobody.

Of course, since it was only one shoe, it was doubly useless.

Yet everyone who learned of this shoe was seized with the desire to own it. Curious travelers with hard money winking in their pockets came from as far away as Doubtful Bay. But the shoe was not for sale.

You're thinking this must have been a remarkable shoe.

People lined up outside the shop just to look in the window. Even the town's mayor (whose name is far too long and important to write out here) felt tempted by it.

He was an impressive man, but not an easy man to im- press. Passing in his carriage, he'd have the coachman slow down so he could catch another glimpse of the famous object, with its sapphires, opals, and moonstones flashing in the sun.

Did I mention the shoe was covered with precious stones?

Precious and semiprecious, and a few (like the beads of Murano glass) merely beautiful. And all of them blue. Blue of every description, from palest aquamarine to clearest azure to dramatic cobalt to assertive navy to deep-thinking indigo.

A blue shoe.

The shoemaker—I should say this right away—was a simple man, nothing remarkable about him at all. Everyone called him Grel, which was his name, or as much of it as anyone bothered to remember.

Grel was neither very short nor very tall. He wasn't particularly thin, nor exactly fat. Neither ugly nor handsome. He had a beard (now threaded with gray), but most Aplanap men wore beards. He was poor, but not poor enough to be arrested.

Did I mention that the poor were arrested in Aplanap? They were. Well, beggars were arrested. You could be poor all you wanted and you'd be left alone. But if hunger forced you into the streets to beg for a coin, large men would come and cart you to jail, and from there, they'd ship you to the north side of the next mountain, a peak so tall its top was perpetually covered in snow and surrounded by swirling clouds.

There were many superstitions about this mountain. It stood in plain sight, and yet you couldn't see the top of it. At night, it was even more mysterious, because the peak pulsed with a dull orange glow. No doubt the light came from the campfires of the beggars condemned to live there, but you know how people are. They'll believe anything. Some said the mountain was really a volcano. Others claimed that trolls hopped about among the crags and spent the nights forging weapons over a great fire. Still others believed the ancient myth about Xexnax, the goddess the mountain was named for. The glow, they said, came from her kitchen, where she roasted the poor doomed souls who'd been sent there.

Whatever the truth, you didn't want to end up on that mountain.

It was a good thing Grel had Hap Barlo, a young boy he'd taken in as an apprentice. A slim thirteen-year-old with nimble hands and likeable eyes, Hap was smart in ways that Grel was not—quick with numbers, sharp at business. More than once he'd saved his absentminded master from ruin.

They were never far from ruin as it was. Cobblers were always needed but badly paid. Grel and the boy often lived on crusts, although they could usually indulge in a slice of schnitzel on Sundays, sitting at a little table in front of the shop, with Grel's dog at their feet. The dog's name was Rauf, since that was the only word the creature knew. Rauf sometimes spoke his word to the passing cats, but he lacked conviction, and the cats paid no attention.

On summer evenings, Rauf would lie contentedly in the dust, one eye closed, the other watching his master and a few old friends playing a game of Plog after the day's work was done. There was something reassuring in the clack of wooden pieces on the game board and the smell of pipe smoke spiraling over Grel's head.

As far as the rest of Aplanap was concerned, Grel might have been invisible. Even regular customers would have a hard time placing him had they seen him outside his shop, without his work apron, walking the tilted streets. Grel didn't mind. He had no desire for recognition. He cared about his sleepy dog, his alert young apprentice, and his art. For he was an artist among cobblers. He might seem vague as he pottered about his shop or rummaged around looking for his glasses, but when it came to work, his concentration was unmatched. The idea of tearing the stones off the fabulous shoe and selling them would never occur to him, any more than he'd tear out his own eyes, especially since, long ago, with excruciating care, he had placed the jewels there himself.

Grel often thought back to that rainy evening when a weirdly tall stranger, his face shadowed in a cowl, had slipped into the shop at closing time. What struck the shoemaker at once were the man's eyes, which glittered with a cold blue fire. Wherever they alighted, they lowered the temperature by ten degrees.

"What can I do for you, sir?" Grel said.

"Ye make shoes, don't ye?"

Grel did not understand at first. The man had a strange accent, a nasal tone, and a voice that started with a grumble in his throat.

"Shoes, you say?"

"Shoes! Shoes! Ye are deafen?"

"Shoes! Yes, the finest."

"Then make me one!"

"Make you . . . one shoe?"

The stranger ignored him. He pulled out a sketch and laid it on the workbench, smoothing its creases with his skinny hand.

One shoe. That's what he wanted. And he paid in advance. Grel watched the heavy coins clink on the wood.

"But that's too much!" he faintly protested.

The man's eyes held him. "Ye complain I pay too much?"

"But it's only one shoe. I should charge you *half* as much, not . . ."

I mentioned, didn't I, that Grel was not a sharp businessman?

More coins clinked on the wood.

"Thinken me," said the stranger in a dark voice, "ye'll earn every groat."

Grel shook his head. It was ten times what he generally received for his work. And only one shoe! What could be simpler?

It was not so simple as he'd imagined. After the stranger had given Grel the measurements, he'd pulled out a velvet purse and emptied it, with a small tinkling sound, on the worktable. Sapphires, tiny blue opals, lapis lazuli, tourmalines, bits of turquoise, topaz, and sky blue quartz glittered in the candlelight, casting a blue glow upward into the cobbler's astonished face.

"Wh-what's this?" Grel stammered.

"This," the stranger replied, pointing a crooked finger, "is to put on the shoe. Use every stone. Leave one out, I will know, and things will go not well."

"I will not leave any out."

"Not one stone."

"Not a single one, I promise!"

The stranger nodded. "I will return."

Grel bowed. "Very good. When should I expect you?"

But he was already at the door, ducking his head under the lintel. Grel was startled to see that the man was wearing no shoes at all, and in the place of toes, he had claws!

Was the shoe for him?

"It will be my masterpiece!" Grel called out as the stranger disappeared in the darkness.

So it was. Never had anyone constructed such a shoe. Even more remarkable than the gleam of the jewels was the daring design itself. From its delicacy of line, it seemed a woman's shoe, if it was meant for a human at all. Whoever would wear it must have an exceedingly odd-shaped foot, thick at the heel, then tapering weirdly to a point. From a certain angle, it looked, in fact, a bit like Doubtful Bay, the glittering watercourse that wound around the base of the mountain and that one could see from any point in town, simply by looking down. Grel began to think of the object as "The Doubtful Shoe." He poured all his artistry into it, staying up nights to get it finished. The result was the most weirdly beautiful shoe ever cobbled. As a last touch, he put his mark, a small backward G, on the tongue of the shoe. He always did this. It was the one touch of pride in a modest man, like an artist signing his painting.

9

For a long time, no one except Grel and his apprentice knew of the shoe's existence. Grel kept it wrapped in brown paper tied with a string on a shelf in the back of the shop. But Hap had helped him make it, fetching special clips and clasps from the local jeweler and thin silk ribbons from the dressmaker, and he itched to tell someone about it. Grel made him promise not to.

"Not even Sophia?" Sophia Hartpence was a girl Hap would have liked to impress. She was a bright little thing with quick blue eyes and definite ideas about everything. Her parents owned a curio shop, Xexnax Knickknacks, at the edge of town.

"Especially not Sophia. She has a brother, and he

has friends. By the end of the week, even the cats would know."

Hap nodded sadly. Grel was right.

Did I mention that the stranger never returned for his shoe?

It made no sense. Had he had an accident? What would keep him from claiming this wondrous feat of shoe-manship?

Sometimes when young Hap was alone in the shop, he took down the package and unwrapped it. The shoe glowed up at him. How much was it worth? he wondered. Who was it intended for? Someone remarkable, no doubt.

Hap wrapped it up again and set it on the shelf.

He was beginning to think no one would wear it at all.

Two

I SHOULD HAVE mentioned something before now about Hap. It's painful to say, because he had so many good qualities, but, well, here it is: Hap was a thief. He'd had to be, in the terrible months after his mother had died, and his father—Silas Barlo was his name, a beekeeper by trade—had given up on life. It was terrible to see. The man had been so cheerful, such a prankster, almost a playmate to his son. Even Hap's friends liked him, and they didn't go in for grown-ups. With his crooked nose and berry-bright eyes, he made everyone laugh.

And he had a voice—such a wonderful tenor voice that people asked him to sing at their parties and weddings. He did it free of charge, for the pleasure of it.

Some of the locals thought him a fool, but Hap knew better. It was just that he was so grateful for his life, simple as it was, that he could not help pulling pranks or breaking into song.

After his wife fell ill, everything changed. Barlo grew gloomy. When she died, he was so distraught he set his bees loose and tossed the hives over a cliff, never thinking of the consequences.

Consequences were quick to arrive: no money to buy bread, and soon enough no honey to put on the bread they couldn't buy. Father and son foraged for blackberries. They ate leaves. Sometimes they caught fish. At first, the townspeople tried to help by hiring Barlo to sing at their parties, but his songs were so mournful that everyone left depressed. Before long, the only singing jobs Barlo could get were at funerals.

He couldn't pay his taxes or his other debts and was turned out of his house.

It was steal or starve, and his son, Hap, had no trouble choosing between them, especially after he discovered his father crouching in the shadow of the Town Hall one afternoon with a can in his hands, begging for coins.

Begging! In Aplanap!

A vision of the goddess Xexnax in her mountain kitchen flew into Hap's mind. He imagined his father turning slowly on a spit over a hissing fire.

In a panic, Hap hustled his father away to the little shelter they'd built at the far end of Xexnax Park, on the outskirts of town. Later that night, he climbed through the window of the clockmaker's shop and took money from the leather pouch behind the workbench.

In the months that followed, Hap became a skillful pickpocket. His conscience bothered him, but the thought of his father begging in the street struck him like a blow to the chest, and he advised his conscience to leave him alone.

One afternoon, he watched the mayor's wife, Ludmilla the Large, leaving a jewelry shop. A woman fond of heavy rouge and heavy bracelets, Ludmilla was counting gold coins and dropping them into a tiny purse. She had no need for a larger one because she seldom paid for anything. The truth is, the townspeople were afraid of their mayor, and their fear extended to his wife. Shopkeepers let her take whatever she wished and cheerfully put it "on her bill."

Jewelers suffered the most, because Ludmilla was obsessed with ornament. Each roll of fat beneath her chin was enlivened by its own necklace. Each sausage-like finger was weighed down by a ring.

Surely, thought Hap, *so fine a lady wouldn't miss a coin or two.* No sooner had she slipped the purse into her pocket than Hap brushed against her and fished it out, hardly noticing the faint tinkle of a bell.

A gloved hand, remarkably powerful for a woman's, slammed down on his wrist and held him like a vise. The purse, with its bell attached, was held aloft for all to see.

Ludmilla's eyes were fierce but her voice soft. "Well, well," she fairly purred, "what have we here?"

The story was huge news in the sleepy town. The *Daily Aplanapian* quoted the mayor's angry denunciation of the

thief and his beggarly father. Both of them, the mayor told the municipal court, deserved to be sent off at once to the north side of the next mountain, never to be seen again.

If it hadn't been for Grel, that is certainly what would have happened. He was fond of the boy and sorry for the father. Of course, he had no money to pay the enormous fine, but he offered to take the boy in and teach him the honest trade of shoemaking.

The mayor seemed undecided whether to be outraged or amused. "Do you *really* think that *I*"—and here he spoke his whole long, unpronounceable name—"the Lord Mayor of Aplanap, would so easily release the thieving urchin who assaulted my *wife?*"

It was widely understood in the town that the mayor was besotted with his wife's beauty. Anyone injuring or even displeasing her would suffer the full weight of the law—*twice* the full weight.

But the assaulted one held up a hand clinking with bracelets. "Just a moment," she said quietly, and whispered in his ear.

"Really?" he murmured.

She whispered some more.

"Are you quite sure, Luddy?" he said. "Think what he's done."

She gave him a look well known to townspeople— The Look That Cannot Be Denied.

"Very well," he said. "If you wish it."

The Lord Mayor cleared his throat, rubbed his hands, and looked out over the crowd. The room quieted as his brow furrowed in thought. He was a virtuoso with his brow, sometimes raising it in mock surprise, at other times lowering it in disapproval. But his most impressive weapon was the large pink wart that stood on his forehead like a lighthouse amid the rough seas of his frowns. It was a thrilling sight, with three shiny black hairs sprouting from its base. There was no winning an argument against it.

"It seems," he intoned, "that my lovely wife, Ludmilla, is inclined to mercy. We will therefore grant Grel's petition, on condition that he provide her with any shoes she asks him to make."

"Agreed, agreed, of course!" said Grel.

"For the rest of her life."

The shoemaker swallowed. "Yes, sir. Well," he said, "at least for the rest of *my* life."

The mayor furrowed his brow so deeply it nearly hid his eyes. Finally, he nodded. "That will be sufficient."

So it was that Hap came to be the shoemaker's apprentice. The boy's father, unfortunately, did not escape his punishment and was sent to Mount Xexnax to serve his life term. The poor man was so disheartened he almost forgot to wave to his son. He certainly wasn't singing.

Months went by. The sun shone cheerily on the mountainside, while far below, the thrashing waters of Doubtful Bay churned like a crash of silverware. The well-scrubbed cobblestones of Aplanap gleamed. Even the chimney swifts, dipping and twirling, seemed to wear a coat of polish on their wings.

The town had the good fortune to be located on a mountain that was protected from severe weather by the taller mountains surrounding it. Tourists were drawn by its cheeses, its quince preserves, and the local folklore about some mountain goddess who lived in a "cave of winds" somewhere. But visitors were especially keen on the cuckoo clocks. They were the pride of Aplanap, with cuckoos so expertly carved you would swear the birds were real.

It was all very quaint and very profitable. Some said that every time a clock chimed, another coin dropped in a cashbox somewhere in this prosperous town. The truth is that some of the town's wealthier citizens were spoiled by the success they enjoyed. An odor of self-satisfaction hung in the air. When a stray beggar was picked up by the police and deported to Mount Xexnax, people simply looked the other way. I heard one woman declare that there *were* no beggars in Aplanap. That there had *never been* beggars in Aplanap.

Grel the cobbler was under no such illusion. He continued making shoes, repairing straps, replacing worn-out soles, but he barely earned enough to survive. Hap did what he could, striking the best deals for his master's work. He was devoted to Grel. Whenever an impatient customer spoke disrespectfully about the shoemaker, Hap burned to speak up and say, *If you only knew!*

But he remembered his promise. Even when Sophia Hartpence came by, he bit his tongue and kept silent about the blue shoe.

Generally a cheerful soul, Hap was well liked by customers—in fact, by pretty much everybody. Sophia made fun of him, and that was upsetting; but maybe, he thought, that meant she liked him, or why would she bother? You could never tell with girls.

When he was alone, though, and especially at night, Hap turned quiet.

Father, he thought, *are you very cold? How are they treating you over there?*

Hap sent his father letters, enclosing a few coins that he'd managed to save—and once a pair of sheepskin boots that Grel had made specially, with velvet lining.

But no letter ever came back. Grel would sometimes find the boy sitting on the three-legged stool outside the shop gazing across the valley at the cloud-covered peak. Even in summer, when geraniums were blooming in the window boxes, the snow on the far mountain didn't melt, and the clouds seldom lifted.

He burned to rescue his father! But how?

Was he a coward? He didn't think so. And he didn't really believe those silly stories about a mountain goddess. Well, in the daytime, he didn't believe them. At night, when the distant peak glowed dirty orange, he had less success controlling his imagination. That's when the terrible Xexnax struck fear in his soul.

While Hap was feeling guilty about his father, Grel was feeling guilty about the shoe. There was no reason he should; he'd done his job well, and the shoe was safely hidden in the back. But when a year had passed and no one had come for it, Grel decided to put a notice in the *Daily Aplanapian* announcing, in the most vague terms, that a certain item was ready for a certain exceedingly tall client and that if the esteemed customer would present himself at a certain shop to collect said item, the proprietor would be greatly obliged.

No one understood a word of this. Probably the person it was intended for would not have understood it either.

But Grel's announcement did not go unseen. The town's mayor, a sharp-eyed fellow, became curious. Who, he wondered, would pay to have such an incompetent message printed? Unless it were a code of some kind. His political enemies, of which he had many, were always plotting against him.

A certain item. A dagger, perhaps? A dagger with a poisoned tip?

Surely not, he thought.

Still . . .

The mayor was the sort who considered his day incomplete if something was going on that he didn't know about; so he sent his nephew around to the newspaper office to learn who had placed the item. When he heard it was Grel, a person of extreme insignificance, he was at first relieved. Clearly, this was *not* a coded message. But what on earth was the shoemaker up to? And why so mysterious? A certain item? A certain exceedingly tall client? What client?

Since it was a slow day for intrigue at the Town Hall, the mayor decided to investigate further. He instructed his nephew, a smirking seventeen-year-old with know-it-all eyes, to snoop around the shoemaker's shop and find out if a particularly large or important order had recently been filled.

The boy found Grel tapping away at a clog and engaged him in conversation. He soon got around to mentioning the newspaper notice, but Grel, although polite, would not say what it was about or who the mysterious client was.

"Couldn't be from around here," said the boy, narrowing his eyes in thought.

Grel said nothing.

"You wouldn't use the newspaper to reach him. You could just knock on his door."

Grel picked up the clog he'd been working on. "I'd better deliver this," he said, and went out, leaving the mayor's nephew standing in the empty room.

The boy stalked out and ran into Hap. "Your master's a very rude fellow," he declared.

"Really? He's always been kind to me."

"He's a fool."

"He's an artist," Hap retorted.

"Artist! He was pounding on a clog."

"You don't know him," said Hap, who couldn't stand having people talk disrespectfully about his master. "If you only knew what he's done!"

"What? Boots for the bricklayer? Sandals for the scullery maid?"

Hap was easygoing enough, quick to see the good, but this fellow was getting on his nerves. "Never mind."

"No, tell me. Maybe he made sandals for that peasant girl you're always sniffing around. What's her name?"

Hap just stared. Should he hit him now?

"Pretty enough," the boy went on airily, "if you go for that sort. Anyway, I can see there's no need for me to wait around. It's obvious what your master does."

"And what is that?"

"Poor, commonplace work for poor, commonplace people."

"You don't know what you're talking about."

"Oh, I think I do."

"My master," said Hap through his teeth, "has created the most amazing shoe in the world!"

"I'm sure he has."

"You don't believe me."

"Of course I do."

This was too much. "Come on," Hap said, and led the older boy to the back of the store. As he undid the package, a soft blue light leaked from the folds in the paper. The mayor's nephew seemed to fall into a trance. His mouth rounded, and his eyes, which were a suspicious green, turned a more honest blue in the strange light.

Shaking himself awake, the boy asked many questions, which Hap answered proudly.

"How much?"

"How much what?"

"How much will the old man sell it for?"

"It's not for sale."

"Well," said the other, his eyes a glittering green again, "we'll see about that."

Hap stood in the doorway watching him hurry away. Something about the encounter gave Hap an uneasy feeling, as if he'd eaten a bad quince—or said too much.

Three

FROM THEN ON, the shoemaker had no peace. The mayor, he of the unwieldy name, insisted on seeing the shoe, and Grel had to bring it out. One did not say no to the mayor of Aplanap.

The great man never traveled without three assistants, but there was no room in the little shop, so he left them to guard the carriage and went in alone. Adjusting to the dim light, he stood scratching his cheek with a manicured finger and gazed down at the cobbler. The cobbler gazed up at him. Their faces were bathed in the glow of the shoe.

"May I?" said the mayor. He pulled a magnifying glass from his vest pocket and bent over the shoe. "A lovely tourmaline," he remarked, scanning the buckle.

"Yes, it is."

"And look at that sapphire!" He frowned. "What's this?"

"Where?"

"The large one on the heel. That couldn't be a diamond."

"Are diamonds blue?"

"No. Well, almost never." His eyes gleamed. "Almost," he murmured to himself, "never."

The great man stood up and patted his vest. "It seems to me that this shoe of yours will make a fine addition to my wife's shoe collection. Not to mention her jewelry collection."

"Oh, I don't think—" the shoemaker began.

"Have it wrapped and sent over this afternoon."

Grel was aware of the fierce-looking wart above the mayor's eyebrow, but he couldn't see it very well. He was still wearing the thick glasses he used for close work. They made everything perfectly sharp nine inches away but a blur beyond that.

"I'm afraid I can't."

The wart trembled. Its three black hairs waved like tiny antennae. "And *I'm* afraid you can't refuse," said the mayor. "It was our agreement that you would make my wife any shoe she liked."

"Oh, and I will. But this shoe was made for someone else. In fact, I've already been paid for it."

"But the owner isn't coming back!"

"He may."

"The goddess of the mountain may come back, too," the mayor snorted, "but she hasn't been heard from in nine hundred years!"

"Still," said Grel, quietly standing his ground, "the shoe is not mine to give you."

"Then I'll buy it," the man stormed.

"It is not mine to sell."

"Blast it! I want that shoe!"

"So I see."

The mayor's heavy brows lowered till his eyes were shadows in a cave. "I can just take it, you know."

Grel looked down and smiled. "I know you are making a joke, sir. You yourself established the penalty for stealing."

The mayor wasn't prepared for this resistance. A little worm of a man defying the Lord Mayor of Aplanap! "I could make life very hard for you," he said darkly, "or very easy. The choice is yours."

Grel knew this was true. He'd seen it happen to others. But how could he sell what was not his? "Any other shoe," he said.

"I don't *want* any other shoe!"

Grel shrugged.

"You *shrug* at me?"

"No, sir."

"I saw you shrug!"

"It was an itch."

The mayor's wart was twitching wildly. Without a word, the man turned and stalked out of the shop, grumbling like thunder.

The next day, Grel received a notice that his taxes had been doubled, and he had been fined for allowing his dog to sleep out in front of the shop, where people could trip over him. Also, it had been noticed that his cuckoo clock was running six minutes slow. There was a fine for that as well.

Hap found his master outside the shop on the three-legged stool, staring out over the valley. "I don't have money to pay these fines," he said, pushing the papers across the table. "They'll shut down my business."

"Shut it down! No!"

"What choice is there?"

"But you'll end up having to beg, and they'll arrest you, and they'll send you . . ." The boy glanced at the cloud-shrouded mountain to the north.

Grel didn't reply.

The two of them were so quiet that Rauf looked up to see if they were still there.

"You're definite about not selling the shoe?" said Hap.

"It doesn't belong to me."

"Yes. But what if the owner never comes back? It's been a year."

Grel was silent.

The boy knew better than to argue. Besides, it secretly pleased him that his master had stood up to the mayor. No one had done that before. "Suppose," he said slowly, "you *don't* sell the shoe but just put it in your window."

"What good would that do?"

"What good? Have you ever heard of advertising?"

Grel looked puzzled. Evidently, he had not heard about advertising.

"It's a way," said Hap, "to let people know the kind of work you do."

"It doesn't sound very modest."

"Leave it to me, master. Be as modest as you wish. Keep doing your work as always. What do you say?"

"I don't understand."

"Probably you shouldn't."

"You really think it would help?"

"Things can't be worse than they are."

"True."

"So, you give me permission?"

Grel looked at the boy a long time.

The difference could be seen right away. No sooner had Hap set the wonderful shoe on a pedestal in the window than passersby stopped to stare at it. There was something hypnotic about the way it glittered in the sunlight and at night glimmered in the moonlight. And if clouds happened to cover both sun and moon, the shoe glowed all on its own, spilling blue light over the sidewalk. Crowds stared as if it were a living thing and might suddenly jump up and walk away by itself.

Soon all the Aplanap matrons wanted their shoes made in Grel's little shop. No one would do but Grel, the man who had created the blue miracle. A shoe without Grel's mark on it, his discreet little backward G, was not worth wearing.

Hap was kept almost as busy as his master, taking orders, raising prices, running errands. After a few weeks, he and Grel had earned enough to pay most of the taxes and fines. Hap even carved a sign and hung it above the door. "The Magic Shoe," it said in bold letters.

"What's that?" Grel demanded. He took off his glasses to see better.

"It's the name of your store."

"Why should I name my store?"

"So everyone will remember it and talk about it."

"Well, take the sign down. It is not modest, and it is not true. I know nothing of magic."

"The fire knows nothing of heat," said Hap. "The rainbow knows nothing of color."

"Take it down."

"What would *you* call your shop, master?"

"Do I have to call it anything?"

"It's advertising."

Grel grumbled. He didn't like the word. "Call it," he said, "'The Shop with the Queer-Looking Shoe That Fits Nobody.'"

Hap laughed. "Master," he said gently, "I think maybe you should leave the advertising to me."

"As long as it's true," he said, returning to his workbench. "And as long as it's modest."

"True and modest," Hap grumbled as he unhooked the sign from above the door.

Four

EVENTUALLY, THINGS SETTLED down a bit, and Grel told his assistant to take the morning off.

"Let me take the fishing pole, master," said the boy. "Maybe I can catch something for dinner."

"Don't tell me you're tired of Finster cheese sandwiches!"

"They're all right if you put enough quince jelly on them."

Grel reached over and mussed the boy's hair. "Even so," he said, smiling, "a nice fish now and then . . ."

"I'll get a big one."

Hap was glad to have a fine, bright morning to himself. He dug some worms for bait, dropping them in a jar with a bit of sphagnum moss, then headed out of town with the pole over his shoulder.

Following the stream, he came to a plateau where the water widened into a pool. He'd had luck here before and wasn't surprised to see several of his friends, also with lines in the water.

Jon Hartpence was there; and Rag, the quince-pickers' son; and Jon's sister, Sophia, who claimed to know magic, although if she did, it wasn't helping her catch any fish. She had shiny ringlets and dirty knees.

"Hello, Miss Sophia," Hap said.

She looked up from the book she was reading. "Oh! Look who's coming, Jon," she called to her brother. "Better hide your wallet!" She never let Hap forget his pickpocketing past.

Jon squinted in Hap's direction. He was subject to headaches, and the bright sunlight wasn't helping. But he never complained, which was one reason Hap prized him as a friend. Jon was also protective of his sister, though you wouldn't know it from the way he talked. Right now, he and Rag were skipping stones across the water.

"I'm sure your money is quite safe, Miss Sophia," said Hap.

"Yes," she said, "since I don't have any. And the fish are quite safe as well, with them throwing rocks in the water."

Rag gave her a disgusted look. "We're having a contest."

"Tell them to stop, Hap," she said, as if he would have influence.

"Why don't you put a spell on us," said her brother, Jon, "and make us stop?"

"Maybe I will!"

"If that doesn't work, you could tell Father."

"Ha-ha."

It was a joke between them. The truth was, their parents were constantly fighting and barely noticed their children at all. Sometimes the fights involved flying objects. They'd long ago gone through their china plates and replaced them with wooden ones that weren't so breakable. How their curio shop, with its delicate trinkets, survived was a mystery.

Hap baited his hook. "Who's winning?"

"Me," said Jon.

"Not for long," said Rag. He flung another stone, using his special sideways throw. It skipped nine times and might have skipped ten except, just then, to everyone's astonishment, a large rainbow trout burst out of the water, caught the stone in its mouth, and splashed out of sight.

"That's quite a spell, Miss Sophia," said Hap, smiling. He cast his line out to the place where the fish had been.

"That wasn't a spell," she said seriously. "That was the goddess."

Hap cocked his head as if he hadn't heard right.

"Some animals are magic. Don't you know that?"

Jon signaled to Hap not to pay attention.

"It's true!" Sophia protested. "It's right here in the book."

Hap checked his bait and cast in a different spot. Nothing.

"Everybody knows," she said, "if you see a raven, you're going on a long journey."

"I have to listen to this all day," Jon said. His hand was on his forehead to shield his eyes.

"And if a turtle crosses your path, you'll have a strong house."

Hap cast his line into a weedy cove where he'd sometimes had luck.

Nothing.

"But it's not every turtle."

"Of course not."

"Different turtles mean different things."

Hap smiled at her happily. Her voice was like a bubbling brook. It didn't much matter what she said.

Sophia watched him. "The fish don't like you," she said with satisfaction. She gave her head a toss, her hair jingling with sunlight.

"And why is that?"

"You have to talk to them."

"Talk to them how?"

She waved away a fly. "You have to say a spell."

"Oh no!" said Jon.

"I'll try anything," said Hap. "I'm so sick of Finster cheese sandwiches . . ."

"Okay." She opened the well-thumbed little book to the middle. "After me, then. By the power of Xexnax!" she declaimed, flinging her arms out.

"By the power of Xexnax," Hap repeated.

"I, Hap the unworthy . . ."

He threw her a look. "I, Hap the unworthy . . ."

"Thief of Aplanap—"

"Okay, that's enough!"

She giggled. "All right, that's not really in the book."

"No kidding."

"We'll do the short version," she said. "Ready?"

He nodded warily.

She flung her arms wide. "By the power of Xexnax! I hereby command the fishies in the brook to come and bite my little hook!"

"That's ridiculous," Hap said.

"Fine. Enjoy your sandwiches."

He sighed but lifted his voice and spoke the words of the spell.

Two seconds later, a violent tug almost ripped the pole out of his hands.

Everybody jumped up shouting as Hap fought the tremendous creature to shore. When it was almost close enough to reach, he caught a brief glimpse of its broad, spiny shell.

Shell?

Suddenly, a huge turtle thrust itself halfway out of the water, swung its furious head to the side like a scimitar, and snapped the line. The monster whirled back under the surface, leaving the children speechless.

"Maybe," said Hap, "we should hold off on spells for a while." He noticed that Sophia looked scared. "What is it?" he said.

"Nothing."

"Was that one of your magic animals? A turtle, right? That means I'll have a strong house."

"Wrong turtle."

"What do you mean?"

"Don't listen to her," said her brother, but even he had stopped throwing stones.

"That was a snapper, wasn't it?" she said.

"The biggest I've ever seen."

She nodded. "And it cut your line."

"You saw it."

"It probably means nothing."

"It means," said Hap, "I lost a hook. Anybody got one I can borrow?"

Rag dug into his pocket. It had a hole in it. All his pockets had holes. That's why his friends called him Rag. He smiled and shrugged.

"Never mind," said Jon. "I've got one."

Before he left, an hour later, Hap did in fact land a respectable trout and pulled it, flipping madly, onto the shale.

"Do you have to go?" said Sophia, watching him wrap his fish in leaves to keep it fresh.

"I'd better."

"He's got to go back to that crazy old shoemaker," said Rag.

"Don't pay any attention," she said. "He's jealous of your fish."

Hap waved a peaceful hand and started up the rock-strewn path to town.

"Be careful!" Sophia called after him.

Hap gave another wave and went on. He felt

unaccountably happy—seeing Sophia had that effect on him, despite her maddening quirks—and he hummed to himself as he climbed the fence onto the town's main street.

Master will be pleased, he thought.

The little shops lay ahead, each one neater and brighter than the next. But something wasn't right. Someone had dumped a dirty bundle on the curb. The streets in Aplanap were always kept whisk-broom clean, and no one left trash in front of their shops.

Coming closer, Hap realized that the bundle was in fact a human being. You couldn't see the person's face under the dirty green blanket, but a crutch was partly visible, and a white hand poked out holding a tin cup.

A beggar! In Aplanap?

"Excuse me, mister," Hap called out, hurrying over. "Excuse me. You can't do that here."

The tin cup swung around in his direction.

"You don't understand. They'll arrest you! They'll send you off to the next mountain!"

The cup didn't move. There wasn't a single coin in it, Hap noticed. Of course there wasn't. Who would risk giving a beggar a coin? It was as serious a crime to *give* to beggars as it was to beg in the first place.

"Come on, sir. We've got to get you out of here." Hap took hold of the beggar's arm, still covered by the blanket, and tried to pull him to his feet.

The blanket fell away, revealing long, matted hair; a dirty face; and a single angry eye. Hap stepped back.

It was a child! A child with one eye!

"Who are you?" he said. "You're not from around here."

No answer. He wanted to look away but looked more closely. He could see now that the rags the beggar wore were the remnants of a dress.

"You're a girl!"

No answer, except a silent shake of the cup. *Unpleasant little creature*, he thought.

The child wound herself in the blanket until only her fierce eye could be seen.

"Don't you understand?" Hap said. "You can't be here!"

The girl's steady gaze unnerved him. Why didn't she say something?

"Where do you live? You need to go home."

She held out the dented cup as if it were a gun.

"Here," he said, exasperated, and took out the trout he'd caught. "Take this back to your parents."

Her eye narrowed. She took the fish, then slowly turned and limped away, leaning on her crutch and trailing the filthy blanket behind her.

"You're welcome!" Hap called after her. *Ungrateful wretch*, he thought.

The girl didn't turn. Finally, she reached a bend in the street and disappeared.

Five

"You did the right thing," said Grel, cutting a Finster cheese sandwich on the diagonal.

"She could at least have said thank you."

"She probably hasn't been taught. What would she know about please and thank you?" Grel poured a mug of warm goat's milk and set it before the boy.

They ate in silence.

"Maybe she's a mute," said Hap.

Grel nodded. "It's possible."

"Where did she come from? Where does she live?"

Grel reached over and mussed the boy's hair. "You've got a good heart," he said.

The next morning, Hap was on a stepladder hanging the new sign over the door. "The Blue Shoe," it said simply. That was the most his master would agree to. No *magical* or *amazing* or *wondrous*.

A small crowd had already gathered in front of the window. In the street, passing carts and coaches slowed and their passengers craned their necks to get a better look. Hap even caught sight of the mayor's ebony and gold carriage rumbling by.

But then he saw something else, and his heart sank. A creature wrapped in a green blanket sat on a curbstone at the edge of the crowd. A thin arm held out a dented cup.

"No, no!" Hap cried, jumping down from the ladder. "You've got to get out of here!"

From a fold in the blanket, a dark eye stared out at him.

Several people in the crowd had turned to look. Soon, he knew, it would be too late. He pulled the child to her feet and hustled her around the back of the shop. "Wait here!" he warned sternly, sitting her down on a stump.

He ran inside to tell his master what had happened but found him deep in conversation with Ludmilla the Large, the mayor's wife. She was here to discuss dancing shoes for her daughter, Edwinna. Seeing Hap, she glared, her rouged cheeks glowing.

"You still have that little thief working for you, I see," she said to Grel.

Grel threw Hap a smile. "Oh, he's turned out to be a wonderful apprentice."

"No more stealing and begging?"

"Not in the least," Grel said with a laugh.

Hap nodded politely and backed away. This would *not* be the moment to ask what to do about a beggar girl. He ducked into the larder and took a fresh, crusty loaf of bread that the baker had given Grel in exchange for a pair of sandals. Then he returned to the child.

"Here," he said breathlessly. He handed her the loaf, noting that it was almost as tall as she was. The girl still kept her head covered with the blanket, but he could make out the glint of her eye. Without a word, she stood and started limping away on her little crutch.

"Wait," Hap said. "Who are you?"

The creature turned briefly toward him, then continued on.

"Where do you live?"

The girl headed toward the street.

"Listen to me," Hap called after her. "You can't come around here anymore. You're putting yourself in danger. You're putting *us* in danger!"

She was gone.

Late that night, a low sound pulled Hap from a dream. It was Rauf growling. Rauf never growled. Immediately awake, Hap climbed from his narrow cot and padded to the front room of the shop. His breath caught in his throat to see a ghostly blue object floating through the darkness.

It was the shoe, his master's wonderful blue shoe. Someone was carrying it to the side window. Someone, Hap realized with a start, was *stealing* it!

"Stop!" he shouted, stumbling forward.

"Rauf!" said Rauf in his loudest voice. *"Rauf! Rauf! Rauf!"*

The shoe moved faster, with a jerky motion. There was a loud crash. Hap grabbed the darkness. It was someone's arm.

"Give it back!" Hap yelled. A moment later, he was spinning backward, sparks dancing before his eyes. His cheekbone throbbed.

The glowing shoe was at the window. Against the dim light from the street, the outline of a tall, thin person was just visible. He had one foot over the sill.

Hap heard a thump, a growl, and a scramble.

"Ow!"

It was a boy's voice.

"Let go, you filthy dog!"

Suddenly, the shoe swung down like a hammer. There was a loud yelp followed by whimpering.

He's hurting Rauf! Hap plunged blindly forward and ran full force into the thief, who let out a grunt and dropped the shoe.

Again, Hap was flung forcibly back, but this time the thief's punch went wild. Hap was back at him in a moment. He became aware of a flickering light and saw that his master, Grel, had come in, holding a lantern.

Hap got a brief look at the intruder's face. It was that smirking boy, the mayor's nephew. He wasn't smirking now; he looked frightened. Giving Hap a shove, he turned and scrambled through the window, hitting his head sharply on the frame.

Hap and Grel watched him run through the street, his boots pounding the cobblestones. Then Hap dropped to his knees to look at the dog, who was still whimpering.

"Let me take a look at that bruise," Grel said.

"Is Rauf bruised?"

"No, you. Your cheek is all swollen."

Hap tenderly touched the place. It felt hot. "I'll be all right. How's the shoe?"

Grel picked it up. A small moonstone had come loose. Easily fixed. Grel looked gravely at his apprentice. "I'm a lucky old man," he said, "to have a brave helper like you."

Hap glowed at the words.

The dog nuzzled the shoemaker's hand.

"And Rauf, too," Grel said.

Six

MORNING SUN GLINTED off trumpets as they blared a triumphant fanfare. It was the Lord Mayor's Annual Birthday Parade, and the street was lined with cheering citizens.

Behind the marching bands strode the municipal guards, in their tightly starched uniforms. Then came a squadron of young girls strewing rose petals—which were promptly swept up by the sanitation police. At last, the mayor's open carriage rolled by, with the great man and his great big wife, Ludmilla the Large, waving to the crowd.

The mayor was dressed in his finest, with all his medals in rows. Even the three hairs on his wart had been washed and curled that morning. As for Ludmilla, she wore so many jewels that the townspeople had to shield their eyes.

Hap and Grel were among the crowd, of course. It was a civic duty to honor the mayor on his natal day, as a policeman had reminded them earlier that morning. Looking around, Hap noticed officials mingling in the crowd, taking notes on who was cheering and who wasn't. Hap started cheering louder than anybody, to make up for Grel, who wasn't cheering at all.

Suddenly, from between the boy's legs, a small, dirty creature darted out in the midst of traffic, just as the Lord Mayor's carriage approached. The crowd gasped.

"No!" Hap cried.

Swathed in a greasy green blanket, the creature stood defiantly in the middle of the street, causing the surprised horses to swerve to a stop and throwing Ludmilla and all her jewelry into her husband's lap. He lay gasping with the wind knocked out of him until his wife managed to climb off and fall back to her seat. He was still woozy as he tried to focus on the filthy lump blocking the way.

From somewhere under the blanket, a thin arm held out a metal cup.

"What's this?" he cried.

"I think," his wife stammered, a little unsteady herself, "it's a beggar!"

"*What!*" boomed the mayor. "In Aplanap?"

"Well, *look* at him!"

He squinted. "I can't see anything under that awful blanket."

"You can see the *cup*, can't you?"

"Of course I can see the cup! Perhaps this unfortunate person is offering us a present of some sort. A humble offering, to be sure, but . . ."

The arm gave the cup a defiant shake.

"Dear," declared Ludmilla, "it's a *beggar*."

He looked at her.

She nodded.

The offender was quickly whisked away and bound over for trial. At some point, it was discovered she was a child—in fact, a little girl, although not a girl that any decent Aplanapian would choose for a daughter. She fiercely guarded her crutch and dirty blanket and would not be persuaded to take a bath. All well-brought-up children took baths twice a day.

The next morning, the girl was led into the columned courthouse, her little crutch making a slow *tock, tock, tock* on the marble floor. Curious townsfolk jammed the back of the chamber, jostling for a view. There wasn't much to see, since the child was still wound in her blanket, which trailed behind her like a queen's train.

The Lord Mayor gazed down from the high bench.

"Your name, child?" he asked, not unkindly.

No answer from the mounded blanket.

"Where do you live? Who are your parents?"

No answer.

The mayor did not want to appear to be bullying a child, especially if its parents should turn out to be taxpayers, but this was insulting.

"Why do you not answer me?"

No answer.

"Are you aware," he said, pronouncing the words slowly, so that even a mental defective could understand, "of the penalty for begging in the streets of Aplanap?"

From the darkness of the blanket came a flash of defiance, but no answer.

The hairs on the mayor's wart twitched dangerously. "I said, do you know the *penalty?*"

No answer.

"Well, I will *tell* you the penalty, you impudent creature. It is banishment to the north side of the next mountain! What do you think of *that?*"

The girl kept her thoughts to herself.

The mayor let out an exasperated sigh. "Would you please remove that filthy blanket so we can see you?"

No movement.

He turned to the guards and nodded. One of them took hold of the blanket, but the girl spun around and bit his hand, drawing blood.

Another guard approached. The girl crouched like a fighter and let out a growl. The man hesitated.

The mayor raised his hand. "Let her be. Clearly, the child is insane. Being insane is no defense, of course, so we must find her guilty as charged."

"*Wait, sir!*" came a voice from the back of the chamber.

"Who speaks?" The mayor shaded his eyes.

Slowly, twisting his cap in his hands, a boy stepped forward.

"It's that horrid little thief!" cried Ludmilla, her several chins trembling. "The one who works for the shoemaker."

"I believe you're right, my dear," said her husband. He turned his narrowing eyes on Hap. "What do you want?"

"Begging your pardon," Hap answered, "but isn't there some other punishment you could impose in this case?"

"Other punishment?"

"Other than sending her off—"

"No there isn't. Now, with your permission . . ."

Hap ducked his head and was about to withdraw. He paused. "But," he began, looking around.

"Are you still speaking?" The mayor's left eyebrow rose dangerously.

"I just thought," Hap said, "there might be a fine or something."

"A fine? Of course there's a fine! But how do you suppose a beggar girl would come up with *ten gold pieces?*"

"Ah, yes," said the boy, nodding, "that is a lot of money."

"Indeed it is. Now, if you'll excuse us—"

"Wait!" cried Hap suddenly. "I'll be right back!" Before anyone could speak, he ducked out of the chamber and ran up the street to Grel's shop.

He arrived, gasping, and called his master's name, but the only response was the wagging tail of Rauf, who'd been wakened from a nap.

"Where *is* he?" cried Hap, forgetting that the dog knew only one word, and not a helpful one. "I've got to find him!" Hap hurried into the back room but found it empty. "I need his permission."

There was no time. The mayor's justice was swift, and the girl might be sent to her punishment at any moment. It would be a death sentence. That wretched little blanket of hers, he knew, was no protection against wind-whipped snow. Nor would her crutch be much of a weapon against Xexnax or whatever monster prowled those desolate slopes.

Anyway, she was deformed. One eye! And a limp. Probably mentally defective as well.

Hap stood before the shop window, staring at the wonderful shoe. He was afraid of very little in this world, but he hesitated. The shoe seemed alive, bathed in ghostly fire.

49

He lifted it carefully. He examined the jewels. The jewels examined him.

Almost any one of them, he thought, would pay the beggar girl's fine.

His eye rested, finally, on a large, sparkling stone attached to the heel. He didn't know much about gems, but this one was a particularly luminous blue. Surely, nobody would notice the absence of one stone. And on the heel. Who looks at the heel of a shoe?

He took hold of it.

Wait, he thought.

He sat down. Rauf wiggled up to him and licked his hand.

You did what you could. You gave her your fish. You gave

her bread. No one expects you to do more. She doesn't expect it herself—and probably wouldn't thank you.

Then he thought of his own case, how Grel had saved him from certain death on the frozen slopes of Mount Xexnax.

What would Grel do?

He'd save her.

He'd save her somehow, simple as that.

Hap gave the stone a tug.

It was fastened snugly. He tugged harder, twisting the stone with all his strength, but Grel had done his work well.

With thumping heart, Hap ran to the workbench and grabbed his master's shears.

As he snipped the thread, he heard a strange sound, like a tiny moan, and the gem fell into his hand.

A great fear swept over him then, like a cool wind—a wind from the north side of the next mountain. Hap closed his hand in a fist so he wouldn't have to look at the stone.

It will pay her fine, he told himself, starting back at a run. *It will pay her fine.*

But what, he wondered distractedly, would *he* have to pay?

PART TWO

Slag

Seven

THE MAYOR GLANCED up. One eyebrow rose high as a question mark. "You again? Why do you keep tormenting us?"

Hap looked around the crowded chamber. "I've come—" he began.

"And you can *go*."

It wasn't easy, with the mayor's wart twitching like that, to remember what he wanted to say. Hap swallowed. "I've come," he said, "to pay the fine."

The room fell silent.

"Excuse me," the mayor said. "You say you've come—"

"To pay her fine, yes."

"And where would you get ten gold pieces?"

"I don't have ten gold pieces."

"Of course not."

"I was hoping this would do instead." The boy reached

out his hand and dropped the gem on the linen-covered table.

The mayor stared at it.

Hap stared at it.

The stone declined to stare back. In fact, to Hap's amazement, it had turned cloudy and gray, like a pebble you might find by the roadside.

"What's this?" said the mayor.

"It's"—Hap's heart was beating fast—"a sapphire? Diamond, maybe?"

The mayor of Aplanap, his gold chain of office jangling on his chest, threw back his head and laughed.

"But it is! It was!"

"It was! That's rich!"

Hap was starting to feel a little sick. "It has to be!"

The mayor moved his face closer to the boy's. "Why is that? Where did you get it?"

"I found it."

"Tell the truth."

The hairs on the mayor's wart waved like conductors' batons. Hap couldn't stop staring.

"The truth!"

Hap swallowed. "I took it from the blue shoe."

A gasp swept through the crowd.

"You *stole* a gem from the shoe?"

"It was only," said Hap, "to pay the girl's fine."

"I see." The man's eyes narrowed. "Well," he said, "I suppose that's to be expected—committing one crime to pay for another."

The boy was silent.

"So where is it?"

"Where is what?"

"The gem you stole. Where is it?"

"You're holding it."

The mayor held up the dull little object. The spectators crowded closer till Hap felt their breath on his neck.

"This is nothing!" The mayor flung the stone on the ground. "But if you've harmed the shoe—"

Immediately, a small hand reached out for the stone and snatched it up. It was the beggar girl.

"Guards!" the mayor barked.

But the child had disappeared in the crowd.

"Catch her!"

There were so many legs, cloaks, elbows, and boots, it was hard for the soldiers to see. The girl was gone.

"Never mind!" cried the mayor. "Fetch me the shoe. And the old man as well."

Three soldiers set off at a run. Two others held Hap's arms. The crowd fell silent. From distant houses, cuckoo clocks began calling out the noon hour. Trees swayed outside the high windows, but inside the hall, the air was heavy and still, laden with the smells of garlic and sweat. Hap was beginning to feel faint.

After endless minutes, the men returned, one of them holding Grel, another carrying the famous blue shoe on a pillow.

"Ohh . . . ," the crowd moaned as they caught sight of it.

The shoe was not blue anymore. It was not any particular color, unless sadness can be called a color. Before it had been amazing; now it was merely peculiar, an odd-shaped, unwearable shoe, covered with knobby pebbles.

The mayor seized it and examined it closely. "The heel!" he exclaimed. "You took it from the heel! Of all the places you could have taken it from . . ."

Hap hung his head. "I thought it would be less noticeable—"

"You destroyed it!" The mayor's eyes rounded in outrage. "Bring me the shoemaker."

The guards shoved Grel forward.

"Did you give this boy permission to take a stone from the shoe?"

Grel had been staring at the shoe but now looked over at Hap. "Did you do this?" he said quietly.

Hap could not lie, not to Grel. "Yes," he said.

Grel sighed.

The mayor had been watching closely. "As I thought," he concluded, giving the table a slap.

"I'm sure he had a reason," said Grel.

"Of course he had a reason! He's a thief. Thieves steal. The boy has confessed as much." The mayor looked over the crowded room. "We've seen enough."

Grel looked up with sudden fear. "Wait."

"No, we will not wait. Guards, take the boy away. Tomorrow morning we'll send him over to Mr. Slag."

"Who is this Slag?" said Grel.

"Someone you'll never meet, if you're lucky."

"And what sentence have you decided on?"

"The usual. Life at hard labor."

"Don't!" Grel cried, his voice stronger.

"It is done."

"He's only a boy!"

"That's a temporary condition." The mayor stood up and adjusted his vest. "Go home, old man," he said. "We have our jobs to do. Yours is to repair the shoe. Mine is to see justice done. Court adjourned!"

Eight

POOR HAP! HE'D certainly got himself into a fine mess this time, and there was no one to help him. The mayor would certainly not listen to Grel. And the other citizens, much as they might like the boy personally, weren't willing to get involved. They were afraid of the angry mayor, his angry wife, and his angry wart.

So it was that Hap found himself crouching in a cell, awaiting deportation. Torchlight gleamed on the stones and cast shadows of jail bars across his face. From distant corridors came the echo of a shout. Then thudding boots. Then silence. Somewhere water was dripping. Hap stood and felt his way around the shadowy cell. No bed, not even a bench or basin.

His foot found a puddle. Leaky pipe, no doubt. He

knelt and scooped water in his hands. He'd had nothing to eat or drink since morning, but the water had a smell to it he didn't trust. *Better thirsty than poisoned,* he thought, drying his hands on his trousers.

He found a corner and squatted down, trying to think. But nothing came except memories: the morning's trial and the shoe. Who would have thought taking one little stone would cause such trouble? The disappointment in his master's eyes still haunted him. Grel's masterpiece, destroyed. Even worse was losing his trust. Grel had taken the boy into his home, and how did Hap repay him?

He closed his eyes, which only accentuated the sound of dripping water. He had never felt so alone.

But then another sound reached him. A bump, or a clunk, from somewhere overhead, followed by scuffling. *Rats in the air shaft?* he thought. Then a louder commotion. He stood up. Whatever the thing was, it was bigger than a rat!

He stared at the dirty ceiling. The metal vent in the middle was shaking.

More scuffling, a dull bang, a groan of metal, and then suddenly the vent gave way and a large object hurtled to the floor.

Hap jumped back in panic as the thing gave out a yowl that echoed down the corridor. He waited, but whatever it was made no further sound. It lay like a lump before him.

He stepped closer, his fists ready.

The thing moaned.

"What are you?" he said, as menacingly as he could.

The creature raised its head. Even in the dark, he could see the shine of ringlets.

"Sophia?"

"Oooh!"

"Sophia, are you all right?"

She frowned, trying to see. "Hap? You mean I *found* you?"

He took her by the arm to help her up. A bruise darkened her forehead. Her smock was torn.

"How did you get here?"

Sophia rubbed her shoulder. She'd landed pretty hard. "The, um . . ." She gestured vaguely. "Jon showed me where the air vents were."

Before she could explain further, the hallway echoed with the clatter of boots.

Guards! They were coming in a hurry.

"What's going on here!" barked the first to arrive. His bare skull gleamed in the torchlight.

Hap gestured upward. "Ceiling. Fell down and nearly killed me!"

A second guard arrived more slowly. A heavy man in need of a shave, he shifted from side to side as he toiled along.

"There's a leaky pipe up there," Hap went on. "Probably weakened the ceiling."

The man lifted his torch higher and peered through the bars.

The other guard gave a grunt.

The bald one turned narrow eyes on Hap. "You have anything to do with this?"

"Does it look like I can reach the ceiling?"

The man glanced around the cell and gave the bars a shake before turning away. Hap listened as the men's footsteps diminished down the corridor.

He'd been sitting cross-legged. Now he slowly got up.

Sophia groaned. "You sure are heavy." She struggled to her hands and knees.

"I don't think they'll be back," Hap said.

"Hope not. I wouldn't want you sitting on me again."

"I'm not *that* heavy."

"You're an ox!" But she was smiling.

It was a nice smile, and he just let it shine for a while. "Sophia, what are you doing here?"

"I came to save you. Oh," she said, remembering. She picked up a cloth bag she had with her. "I brought some things."

Out tumbled a length of rope, a round of pumpernickel, a small knife, and a pair of wool-lined boots. Hap picked up the boots. There was Grel's little backward G on the tongue. "He made these for me?"

"He worked all day on them. Just in case."

"In case?"

"I couldn't get you out of here."

So, Hap thought, *the master has forgiven me.* Relief flooded through him, even as a further thought occurred: *I don't deserve it.*

"Right now," he said, "I'm more worried about getting *you* out."

Sophia looked up. "You were supposed to climb the rope. But now that we're both down here . . ."

"Yes."

She brightened. "What if I stand on your shoulders?"

"What will that do?"

"I could reach the ceiling and climb up. Then I could lower the rope to you."

"All right."

Climbing onto Hap's back was easy enough, but standing on his shoulders proved a wobbly business, and Sophia kept slipping.

"Clamp your feet around my head," Hap whispered as she tried again.

She stood up and pressed her ankles against his ears. That made it hard for Hap to hear, but at least Sophia didn't fall. In a quick movement, she stepped on Hap's head and grabbed a ceiling joist. From there, she pulled herself up.

"Did it!" she gasped, looking down from inside the hole in the ceiling.

"Great!" Hap was rubbing his ear where Sophia had kicked it.

"Now grab on to the rope."

Hap stayed where he was. "You go on."

"What are you talking about?"

"I don't want to be rescued."

"*What!* Hap, you come here right now and grab this rope! Are you crazy?"

"Can't do it."

Her face was a conflict of bewildered anger. "What are you talking about?"

"Don't you see?" he said. "This is perfect. They're sending me to Mount Xexnax."

"You call that perfect?"

"That's where my father is. They're sending me to rescue him and bring him home."

"You'll just go and rescue him."

"Absolutely."

"And bring him back home."

"Why not?"

"Happily ever after."

It occurred to Hap that Sophia wasn't quite with him on this. But he was determined. "Sophia, you should go now."

"Not without you."

"I'll be all right," he said. "I have bread, so I won't starve; boots, so I won't freeze; a knife and rope—"

"So you can stab and hang yourself. Hap, please! Think!"

He shook his head. "I've got to find him."

"You don't know!"

"What do you mean?"

"You saw that turtle."

"You mean the one—"

"It cut your lifeline."

"Sophia, it was a *turtle*."

"It was a *snapping* turtle. The death bringer."

"The what?"

"You don't know anything, do you? It's right there in the book."

"Sophia, you got that book from your parents' store. They sell hundreds of them to tourists. It's not real."

"It's the death bringer, and it'll cut short your life if you go to that mountain."

"I don't believe in that stuff."

A warm droplet landed on his wrist.

"Come on," he whispered, "I'll be all right."

"You better be, you big lug."

"I will."

"Promise."

"Sure."

"You've got to say it."

"I promise I'll be okay."

"By the power of Xexnax."

"Sophia—"

"Say it!"

"By the power of Xexnax."

She gave him a last look, and then her face disappeared. He listened as the rumbling in the air duct grew fainter. Finally, there was no sound at all, except the slow drip of water in the darkness.

Nine

No ANNOUNCEMENT HAD been made, but dozens of towns-people gathered in the public square the next morning. They may not have come to Hap's defense, but they did come for his send-off. You may suspect, as I do, that they felt guilty for all the times they had seen a beggar and turned their eyes away. Here was a boy who had *not* turned away, and he was paying for it.

The mood in the square was so somber you'd have thought they were here for an execution. Grel was among them, and Rauf the dog, panting happily at his feet. Also Hap's friends Jon and Rag. Rag's parents were there, in their patched overalls. They'd gotten permission to take the morning off from quince picking.

No sign of Sophia.

Grel watched as a wooden cage was set in the back of the mule cart, among kegs of ale, rounds of cheese, and sacks of apples and parsnips. Finally, the boy was led out, his small satchel over his shoulder and his hands tied before him. He squinted at the knife-bright sun. The size of the crowd surprised him, and he threw them a jaunty smile.

"God bless you!" called an old woman.

"Don't let them push you around!" shouted Hap's ragged friend, Rag, waving a fist.

"Come back to us, you hear?" cried another.

"I will!" Hap called, stepping into the cart.

At the sound of Hap's voice, Rauf lifted his head. His whole hindquarters wiggled. *"Rauf!"* he said. *"Rauf! Rauf!"*

Hap looked over and saw Grel. Their eyes met, and Hap mouthed the words "Thank you."

Grel nodded. He saw the sheepskin boots on the boy's feet and wanted to say something, but he was slow when it came to words, and by the time he'd found them, the guards had pushed Hap into the cage and the moment was gone.

The driver was a woman—though you might be forgiven for not realizing it right away—dressed in greasy overalls and blue work shirt, her hair held tight under a woolen cap. Broad-faced and sturdy, she was the sort you often saw in the orchards at quince-picking time. She turned and looked at the guard.

The man snapped a padlock on the cage and stepped

back. With a flick of a long stick on the mule's back, the cart lurched into motion.

Hap made a grab for the bars to keep his balance. He saw the town growing smaller, the faces receding. Several people waved, but he was not sure anymore who they were. It came to him that he was leaving Aplanap for the first time in his life—and perhaps the last.

"Everybody comfy?" the driver called over her shoulder. Her voice was like dirty sand.

Hap didn't reply. He was slumped in the back of the cage, his head in his hands.

"Feelin' a little mealy, are ya?" the big woman called to him. "Happens to everybody. It'll pass."

After following the paved road awhile, the driver pulled hard to the right onto a narrow wagon track that led down steep inclines and tight curves toward the wild side of the mountain. Few people took this lane, and it was not well kept up. The driver had to steer around rocks that had tumbled onto the path.

From his cage in the back, Hap could see where they'd been, not where they were going, so he was unaware of how close they were getting to Mount Xexnax until its shadow fell across the wagon and the temperature suddenly dipped.

He had no preparation when the cart lurched to the right, flinging him against the bars and dislodging a large sack of apples, a crate of pickaxes, and a rolled-up carpet. If it hadn't been for the cage, he'd have been crushed.

"Sorry 'bout that one," shouted the driver.

"It's all right," Hap called back.

The woman grunted. With all the rocks to watch out for in the road, she had no time for talk.

But then she gave another grunt. Or did she? It didn't sound like her voice, and it didn't sound like it was coming from the front.

It was coming from the carpet!

Hap reached through the bars and unrolled it partway. From there, it began unrolling itself. Finally, out tumbled a very upset-looking girl with dust-smeared cheeks and disheveled hair.

Sophia winced. "That hurt," she said.

"You!"

She held a finger to her lips.

"What are you doing here?" he stage-whispered.

"Giving you another chance," she whispered back. She reached through the bars and started untying his hands. In the midst of it, the wagon lurched sideways, and she was thrown headfirst against the side of the cart. "Oooh!" she groaned.

"Sorry," called the driver. "Didn't see that one."

"That's okay," Hap answered, shaking loose from the rope. He turned to Sophia. "Didn't I tell you I didn't want to be rescued?" he breathed.

"I thought you might change your mind," she whispered back.

"Not before I find my father."

"Okay. So I've got a second plan." She looked around, as if the bag of apples might be listening. "I'll help you rescue him."

He shook his head. "Too dangerous."

"You mean, for a girl."

"I'm not going to argue with you."

The shadow of the mountain had deepened as the wagon wound its way toward Doubtful Bay. The wind went from cool to cold.

"You really *should* let me rescue you," said Sophia, staring at the cliffs before them.

"You're looking at the mountain?" said Hap, holding his thin jacket closed.

She nodded. "Actually," she said, "I think it's looking at *me*."

"It's telling you to go home."

"I know. But I'm not going to."

"But you have no warm clothes, no . . ."

She dug inside the carpet, pulling out a wool coat for each of them. She also had a compass, her book of *One Hundred Easy Spells for Beginners*, and a slice of schnitzel, cooked specially by Grel.

Hap had nothing to say. Nor did he try to argue as she slipped a coat to him through the bars. She put on the other one herself, then proceeded to cut up the meat, handing him several slices.

He had to admit, it tasted wonderful.

"We'll save the rest for later," she said, wrapping it up.

Hap heard a distant murmur amid the moan of wind. "The bay," he realized aloud.

The wagon bumped from the packed dirt of the road onto a wooden dock. The slap of water was louder now.

"Here we are!" the driver sang out, pulling the cart in a semicircle.

Sophia ducked under the carpet.

From this new angle, Hap could see the thrashing water and, beyond, rising in the freezing mist, the shrouded cliffs of Xexnax.

"Now what?" he called over the noise of the waves.

"Now we wait," the driver shouted. "The ferry's coming."

"Ah."

"Yes," she went on, turning around, "so this'd be a good time for your friend back there to hop out. If she's quick about it, she can make it to town before nightfall."

Hap started to speak but stopped. Lies wouldn't work.

"Come on out, missy," said the woman. Her face was plain as a shovel, but her look was not unkind.

Slowly, Sophia emerged.

"Off you go. You heard me. Scat!"

"I can't."

"What do you mean? You very well *can*."

"He needs me. Without me, he'll die on that mountain."

The driver frowned, taking in the odd idea that this flimsy thirteen-year-old could be of help to anybody. "Oh, he won't die," she said carelessly. "Not right away."

"I don't want him dying *at all*."

"Everybody dies sometime. Even Jack—that's my mule here—he won't be around forever."

"Hap is not a mule!"

Something like a smile cracked the driver's face. "Tell me, missy," she said, "just how were you thinkin' to help him—I mean, aside from untying his ropes?"

Sophia looked down. "I don't know yet. I'm learning some magic."

"Magic! Why didn't you say so?"

"I'm serious!"

"She's got a book," Hap explained. "She's been practicing."

"Practicing!" The woman made a face. "You see this mountain? Take a good look. It's not a place to practice."

"She's right," said Hap.

"You'll die like her dirty old mule!" the girl shot back.

"Hey!" said the driver. "Don't you go insulting Jack."

A distant whistle reached them from far out in the bay. They all looked. The wind was whipping up white-caps, and in the middle of it all, a boat struggled toward shore.

"That's my husband out there," said the driver.

"Really?" said Hap. It was hard for him to think of this large, rough woman as married.

"Three times a day he makes the crossing. A braver one you'll not find."

For some seconds, they all stared out at the snub-nosed ferryboat and the waves dashing against it. At times, it looked as if it might capsize, but it always righted itself.

"What would you do," said Sophia slowly, "if you saw him getting into trouble out there?"

"May lizards bite your tongue, young lady!"

"Would you just sit here on your wagon and watch?"

"What's the matter with you? Sit and watch? If my Ulf was in danger?" She made a gesture of disgust.

"You'd find a way to help?"

"Of course! If I had to swim out there myself!"

Sophia didn't say more. The woman gave her a hard look. "I see what you're about," she said, "and it won't work."

"I'm not about anything."

"Listen. You're a child. That mountain will eat you up."

A second whistle interrupted them. It was the ferry-man calling for his wife to make ready the ropes. The boat was quite near now.

The woman shook her head. "I can't send you to your death."

"But you don't mind sending my friend!"

"I can't help that. It's my job. Now, get off of this wagon. Ulf won't be so gentle about it, I'll tell you that."

"No!"

"Do I have to throw you off?"

"If you can!"

The big woman got up and started toward her, the wagon swaying under her weight.

"Stop it, both of you!" cried Hap, gripping the bars of his cage. No one was listening.

Sophia stood up. "By the power of Xexnax!" She held her skinny arms out to her sides and rotated them in tight circles, her eyes blazing with concentration.

The woman paused, caught between amusement and puzzlement.

Sophia muttered some phrases that neither Hap nor the driver could make sense of. They seemed composed largely of *g*'s and *r*'s, with some *q*'s thrown in.

Suddenly, there was a loud crack, and then the wagon gave a downward jerk and tilted dangerously, throwing the woman off balance and nearly dumping the provisions onto the ground.

Hap looked around, amazed.

"The dock!" the woman called out, looking over the side. "I told Ulf a dozen times to fix that rotted plank."

"It was magic," declared Sophia.

"I admit," said the woman, "your timing's pretty good."

A shout reached them over the turmoil of water. A male voice, not very pleased: *"Hwaet! Ic commin am!"*

Hap gave his head a shake. "What did he say?"

"He's coming in. It's Auki talk. Don't you know anything?"

She turned to Sophia. The girl was sitting cross-legged. "I'm staying," Sophia said flatly.

The woman sighed. "You want to die that much?"

Sophia didn't reply.

The driver gave her a long look. "You better get back inside that rug," she said. "Ulf's not so tenderhearted as me."

Sophia jumped up.

"Quick, now," the woman said severely. "Get down and stay well out of sight, or it's over."

"Wait a minute," said Hap, turning from one to the other. "Nobody asked me—"

"And nobody will," the woman snapped. "You sit and behave!"

Ten

So THAT'S HOW it stood as the ferryboat came in. Sophia was burrowing into the rug, and the mule driver was down off the wagon, uncoiling the mooring lines. She and the ferryman shouted incomprehensible directions to each other as the boat tied up and the gangway lowered.

The seaman coming down the ramp was a strange sight. For one thing, he was noticeably, even drastically, shorter than Hap. He couldn't have been much more than three feet tall!

Under his wool watch cap sprang a full beard, wildly tufted eyebrows, and—was it possible?—a *bluish complexion*. It was just a tinge, really, nothing obvious, but even his hands and forearms had the same light blue tint, as if he'd been dipped in a vat of moonlight. Hap's eye caught the glint of a metal whistle hanging from his neck. It swayed back and forth through the forest of chest hair poking from the top of his shirt.

Ulf, the woman had called him. Could she possibly have meant *elf?* Hap had always thought of elves as slim, nimble creatures out of children's stories. There was nothing elfish about this fellow, tough as blue gristle, striding toward the wagon.

As he came closer, Hap noticed something else peculiar about him—his nose, long as a crooked finger. It seemed to affect his speech, because his words came out nasal: "Haefte nic mare than this, Mag?"

"That's it. A light load for you."

Ulf humphed. He noticed Hap staring. "Hwaet ir loken?"

Hap looked to Mag for help.

"He said, 'What're you lookin' at?' It's a fair question."

"I see." He turned to Ulf. "Excuse me, but are you an elf?"

The creature gave a laugh like the bark of a dog. "Elf! Horen ye, Mag?"

"I heard. But look here, talk so he can understand you. He's just an ignorant human boy."

"All right," he said, switching to human talk. "But he must know there bin nic such ones as elves. Knowen he no thinge?"

"Sorry," said Hap.

"Supaerstition."

"Exactly what I thought."

The seaman grunted. "You thinken this bin an fairy tale? Elves! By gar!"

"Sorry."

He let down the back of the wagon and climbed up to inspect the cargo. "I be but a poor Auki, tryin' to earn a livin'."

"Of course." Hap's words got caught in his throat. "*What* did you say?"

"*Auki*. Know ye nic anything?" Ulf hoisted two bags of parsnips, each as big as himself, gave them a rough shake, and flung them down again.

"Have a care," said Mag. "You know how Slag gets if anything's damaged."

"*Slag!*" he spat, accompanying the name with a gob of phlegm.

"Let me give you a hand with that rug," she said.

"Nan, nan, Mag." He began unrolling the carpet. As he did, he leaned confidentially toward Hap, muttering a bagful of gutturals the boy didn't understand.

"What did he say?"

Mag sighed. "He said you gotta look in everything. He said last month he found a knife somebody'd snuck inside a pie."

"Ay," assented Ulf. He continued unrolling. The edge of Sophia's dress poked out.

"Ulf! Quick!" Mag cried.

"Hwaet?"

"Just remembered. The back wheel! I think it busted through the dock."

"Sartain, luf, when I'm done here."

"No!" said his wife, clamping a heavy hand on his. "First the wheel. *I'll* take care of this."

Ulf sighed and got to his feet. "A piece of advice, son," he said to Hap. "Do ye nic ever marry an mule driver. They be far too particular."

"*Ulf!*"

"Ic gan!"

As soon as he'd climbed down, Mag unwound the carpet until Sophia's foot, then arm, then head appeared. The girl looked scared.

"Still want to go through with this?" whispered Hap. She nodded.

"Quick!" said Mag. "Behind the parsnips!"

Without a word, Sophia scrambled over the sacks and disappeared, just as Ulf came around the side of the wagon.

"Right ye were," he said. "Quite a work ye gedone on that wheel."

"I did?" said Mag.

"And eke the dock. What you carrying there? Elephants?"

Mag chuckled. "Just a couple of squirrels."

"Hwaet?"

"Don't bother yourself. Get the wagon loaded."

Ulf nodded and set to work, muttering, "Some heavy squirrelen."

Minutes later, the prison wagon was blocked in place on the aft deck.

"Cast off!" Ulf shouted, and he and Mag, pulling hand over hand, dragged in the heavy ropes and wound them in coils. The ferry floated out in the current.

After a bit, the mule was given hay and water. Even Hap was let out of his cage. Almost immediately, he fell against the gunwale as the boat pitched. Struggling to his feet, he made for the bow. Mag was already there, leaning against the rail.

Ahead lay Xexnax, and the closer they got, the darker its shadow, the colder the wind, the rougher the waves. Hap made a wild grab for the railing as the ferry shuddered upward on the back of a surge. "Can I ask you something?"

"Too many questions."

Hap caught a fistful of spray in his face. "Have you ever run across a prisoner named Barlo?"

She frowned. "When was he sent over?"

"One year, seven months, twenty-three days."

"Kinfolk?"

"My father."

She nodded.

"He's not very tall," Hap went on. "Taller than your husband, though."

"Most are."

"Not blue."

"Most aren't."

A couple of years ago, Hap would have described his

father as the biggest jokester in Aplanap. "You might re-member him," he said, "as the saddest man you ever saw."

"That so?" She looked over her shoulder at Ulf, who was at the windlass, his hair wild as he struggled to steer between waves.

"So," said Hap, "do you remember him?"

"It was a long time ago," she said.

"Think."

She tilted her head to look him over. "I'll give you a hint, free of charge. Go easy on the thinking. Sometimes it's smart to be dumb."

He looked at her.

"Safer," she said, "especially where you're going. As for your dad—"

Just then, a loud whistle—*peee-weee!*—cut through the air. A few seconds later, a faint answering signal came from shore.

"Gettin' ready to come in," Mag said.

"What about my dad?"

"Afraid I can't help you there."

"What about Sophia? What should I do about her?"

"Nothing."

"But—"

"I've an idea or two."

Hap saw that she wasn't going to say more. The mountain was close now. At first, it was nothing but a vague blue wall. Then he could make out a dock, dimin-ished by haze, and several people hurrying about.

His eyes traced the mountain's flank until the blue

blurred into gray. He looked still higher. The gray disappeared into clouds. *Snow clouds*, he thought, *hanging like a veil of secrecy over the summit.*

To him, they looked neither light nor dark. They were the color of fear.

Eleven

SEVERAL SOLDIERS AND dockworkers were waiting as the boat tied up. Not a blue face among them, Hap noted, and everyone was normal-sized. One of the soldiers was taller than normal.

Jack the mule was hitched up, and Mag coaxed him down the gangway. Hap was locked in his cage.

"This all you got for us?" said the tall soldier. "A kid?"

"That's it."

"What good is he?"

Mag threw him a look.

The man gave the mule a slap on the rump, and they started off. The soldiers had their own wagon and followed behind. The tall one started a raucous song and the others joined in, laughing and banging out the rhythm with their feet. Not one of them could carry a tune. But there was something odd: Hap recognized the melody. Yes, and the words, about the joys of wandering through the Aplanapian countryside. His father used to sing it as they strolled through the woods, years ago. Hap had always assumed his father had made it up.

He wished they'd stop singing it.

The wagons wound up a steep road, past stands of pines and piles of boulders. The higher they went, the fewer the trees and the larger the stones. Hap buttoned his new woolly jacket to the top. The temperature kept dropping, and the wind made his forehead ache. They never had winters like this in Aplanap, he mused. And it wasn't even winter!

Before long, the first snowflakes began twirling down. Hap held his hands over his ears. He was glad Sophia was inside the carpet; Mag had seen to that during the confusion of landing.

The snow came harder, and the mules were having trouble keeping their footing. Hap could barely see the other wagon, though it was close behind. His hair clicked as he ran his hand through it. *Icicles*, he realized.

Quite suddenly, the visibility was down to nothing. They had entered a cloud. Not the soft sort of cloud you read about in children's books. This cloud *bit*.

"Ach!" Hap cried, feeling the first pricking of ice shards. The rest of the way, he cowered at the back of his cage, his coat pulled up to cover his head. It's possible he fell asleep, because he lurched in panic at the groan of the backboard being lowered.

A man stuck his face next to the cage. An extinct pipe hung from his mouth, and his brows were freighted with frost. "Not dead yet?"

Hap was too cold to answer.

"Well, give it time, give it time."

The provisions were unloaded, and Hap's cage was set down on a snowbank. The guard snapped open the lock, and Hap clambered out into knee-high snow. He saw no sign of Mag, but through the icy wind, he made out a fieldstone house with steps leading up to a porch. Carved above the doorway were the letters XCC.

"Is that where I'm staying?" he asked.

"What, in Xexnax Command Central? No, my friend." The guard took the pipe from his mouth and put it back again. "That's where you meet Mr. Slag."

"Who?"

"Come on." He grabbed Hap roughly by the arm and marched him up the steps into the sudden warmth of the house.

Hap looked around warily, taking in the imposing rolltop desk that dominated the room. Above it hung an equally imposing portrait of the Lord Mayor of Aplanap—minus the famous wart.

A creaking sound made him turn. Two men he hadn't noticed sat on a bench along the wall. One of them glanced briefly at the boy, then back at the floor, as though he were of no interest. They seemed to be waiting for something. From the looks of them, it wasn't anything good.

"Better sit," the guard said. "Could be a while."

Hap took a place at the other end of the bench. His hair was soaked with ice melt, trickling down the back of his neck. His mind wandered, drowsy. It was almost too hot in here, yet there was no fireplace or stove. That's when a steady, low whooshing sound caught his attention. The source of it, he realized, was a metal pipe by the baseboard. That's where the heat was coming from.

Curious, he thought, though he was not really curious. He just wanted to be away from here.

Why had he allowed Sophia to come to this horrible place? Somehow he had confidence in Mag, the mule driver. Mag would take care of her. Hap's frown gradually relaxed.

With an icy rush, the door burst open, and several workers came in bearing provisions. They laid them on the floor, as if for inspection. Among them was the rolled-up carpet.

Sophia!

Hap was suddenly alert. He had to get her out of that carpet!

Too late. A door to the back opened and two soldiers strode in, followed by a tall man in his forceful forties, holding two black shepherd dogs on a chain wrapped around his wrist. He carried a heavy ledger book and wore a snappy-looking hat with the front brim turned down and the back turned up. His features, from what Hap could see under the hat's shadow, were composed entirely of right angles, and his eyes were a cold green.

The two unfortunates on the bench jumped to their feet, and then Hap got up as well. In the presence of such a presence, it seemed the thing to do.

One of the big dogs swung its heavy head in Hap's direction.

"Well," said the man crisply, "here's a sorry bunch." He flopped the ledger book onto the desk as his eyes narrowed on the men. "What do you have to say?"

One of them took half a step forward. To take a whole step, it seemed, would have been too daring. Besides, it would have taken him closer to the dogs. "Sorry, Mr. Slag. It won't happen again."

"Why did it happen at *all?*" His voice rose with the question.

"We was hungry, sir."

"Hungry."

"Yes, sir."

"So you waltz into the galley and stuff half a dozen potatoes in your pockets."

The men looked at the floor.

"Well, you'll be hungrier soon enough. For the next week, there'll be no lunches in Portal Three. Do you understand?"

"Yes, sir. Thank you, sir."

"You can explain to your comrades why they're eating less."

Hap stared at the men. What was this "Portal Three"? Did they know his father?

"Now, out of my sight!"

The men shuffled away, and the door closed. Hap turned his eyes to the man called Slag. He couldn't help staring. The mayor of Aplanap had his hypnotic wart. This man had green eyes that looked sharp enough to cut emeralds. There'd be no way to deceive him.

"And this one?" said the man, turning to the guard.

"The prisoner."

"The prisoner. Do they think we run a nursery?"

"No, sir."

"His crime? Let me guess. Begging for a bottle of milk."

"Actually, sir, he was caught stealing."

"Stealing."

"So it seems."

Slag gave his hat brim an irritated tug. "Stealing or begging. Can't anyone in that town do something original?"

"I'm sure I don't know."

"I'm sure you don't. At least they've sent our provisions." He nodded to one of the soldiers, who hurried forward and began unrolling the carpet.

"Don't!" Hap blurted.

The soldier paused. Slag's eyebrow made a tiny mountain peak. Even the dogs looked over.

"I—I mean," Hap stammered.

Slag waited several long seconds. "What's your interest in my rug?"

"I thought it looked like, um, one my uncle had."

"A thief who can't lie. Not very promising."

Hap stood silent.

"What have you hidden in there? Never mind. We'll
know soon enough."

The soldier unrolled the carpet the rest of the way:
a colorful piece, with reds and greens, and blue roses in
the corners. But no girl. Not of any description.

Mag, Hap thought gratefully.

There was, however, one small, limp bit of pink cloth.
Slag held it up. "Yours?"

Hap shook his head.

"What would a girl's sock be doing here?"

The boy shrugged.

"We've caught people being smuggled *out* of here,"
Slag mused. "But I don't recall people being smuggled *in*."
He turned to the soldier to his right. "Have the base
searched! We're looking for a girl—or short woman."

The man saluted.

"And bring that ferryman in. I want to question him."

"Yes, sir!"

"Never trust a Blueskin. Wait a minute!" he called out.

The soldier paused.

Slag held the little sock up to the dogs' noses. They
growled deep in their throats, then let out little yips and
moans of impatience. "Take the dogs. They've got the
scent now. They shouldn't have trouble finding her."

"Yes, sir!" Bracing himself, the soldier took the leash. The dogs were almost uncontrollable with excitement, their sharp toenails scrabbling about on the wood floor as he led them out.

Hap watched the door snap shut.

Slag came to the front of the desk to watch the sacks and packages being opened. That's when Hap noticed the man's shoes. Boots, rather. Soft, buff-colored sheepskin, lined in velvet.

"Where did—?" Hap began, then caught himself.

"Are you addressing me?" said Slag.

"It's nothing," said Hap.

"You seem to be admiring my boots."

Don't say anything, Hap told himself severely, remembering Mag's warning: *Sometimes it's smart to be dumb.*

Slag's eyes glinted. "Come closer. It seems we have the same bootmaker."

"Do we?"

"Even the same insignia. See it? The little backward G?"

"I hadn't noticed."

"Is this one of the things you stole?"

Hap started to deny it, then caught himself. "Yes, sir."

"At least you've got taste." He consulted a list, then scratched the back of his head, under the upturned brim. "Barlo, it says here. That your name?"

"Yes, sir."

"Do you, by any chance, have a relative named Silas?"

"He's my father. I believe you're wearing his boots."

"I resent the implication."

"I only meant—"

"A thief accusing me of stealing! It's funny, really."

"Yes, sir."

"You can take *your* boots off right now! You won't be needing them where you're going." Slag turned to the guard. "See if they can use this lunatic in Portal Four, Section Nine."

"Section Nine, sir? There's just Blueskins down there."

"That's right. At his size, he should fit right in."

"Whatever you say."

Slag folded his arms. "You disapprove."

"No, sir. Well, it don't seem right, humans doing Auki work."

"Perhaps you'd like to take his place."

"Oh no, sir!"

Slag's smile was the narrowest of slits. "Good," he said. "Now get him out of here!"

Twelve

You will have noticed our story has taken a darker turn. It's likely to get darker yet. Can't be helped. We've got to follow our hero wherever he takes us, even if he hasn't the faintest idea where that is.

Hap Barlo didn't see his story as dark. It would be natural, with the black mouth of a mine entrance looming ahead, to feel despair, even panic, but Hap felt only excitement. He was getting closer to his father. He might see him any moment!

The guard poked him with a pole, and Hap took a seat at the back of a low, roofless train car behind a half dozen stoop-shouldered men. One of them, with a hound-dog face smeared with grime, turned to look at him.

"New, are ya?"

Hap nodded.

"Well, keep your head down."

"Keep my head . . . ?" The rest was lost in the groan of metal as the car jerked into motion and started along the flimsy-looking track, straight for the entrance. The opening was low, no more than four feet high, and the car slid through like a deck of cards into a narrow drawer.

A howling darkness engulfed him, relieved every few seconds by the dim glare of a phosphorous torch set in the wall. As the speed picked up, Hap kept his eye on the jags of stone whizzing inches above his head. The wind was cold against his face but grew warmer as the car wound steadily downward, following the sloping track. After what must have been a mile, it slowed and coasted to a stop.

It was a scene from a strange underworld. Odd, human-like creatures, short and swarthy, hopped about in the torchlight, their ankle chains jangling as they banged on machines, bored holes with whining drills, and shouted at one another in a language Hap didn't understand.

"Who's Barlo?" called the driver.

"I am, sir."

"You get out here."

The worker in front of Hap watched as the boy struggled from his seat. "You get on somebody's bad side?" he said.

"What do you mean?" Hap stepped out and found he couldn't stand up all the way.

"Startin' you workin' with Blueskins!" The man shook his head.

"With who?"

"Is that Mr. Barlo?" came a voice from the darkness.

Hap looked around but saw nothing.

The train car, meanwhile, ground its gears and started down the track, carrying the men away to the next work-station. When the taillight had disappeared, Hap was aware of a sudden silence. Not quite silence. The air was laced with the faint trilling of birds.

In a mine?

"Mr. Barlo, is that you?" came the same smooth voice, bouncing off the rock walls till it seemed to come from everywhere at once. A metal pipe, just like the heat pipe in Slag's headquarters, projected from the wall. Was the voice coming from there?

The boy glanced around. All work had stopped. The Aukis were no longer banging or shouting as before. They were staring at *him*, a human boy hunched over to avoid hitting his head.

"Hi there!" ventured Hap, nodding at the nearest worker.

No response.

"They won't talk to you," came the voice from the shadows. "Not most of them. I'm the fellow you want to see."

Hap peered into the dimness. The glow of a cigar caught his eye. Then he made out the curve of a *rocking chair*, of all things, and in it a man with an impressive mustache, the ends waxed and twirled to upturned points. He wore a velvet jacket, sipped an iced drink, and in general looked as if he belonged at a party, not in a filthy mine overseeing Aukis.

The first thing Hap thought was, *How do you get ice in your drink a mile inside a mountain?* "Hello, sir," he began. "Nice to meet you."

"Yes, quite. We don't see many of our kind here. And likely lads such as yourself are rare indeed." He touched a finger to his mustache to check that the point was sharp. "We will strive to make your stay here a pleasant one."

He reached over to touch a golden cage hanging from a stand, making it swing back and forth. "I think they're hungry. Would you mind?" He held up a small box of seeds.

That's when Hap saw the two birds, yellow with dark stripes on their wings, hopping in the cage. He took the seeds and shook some into a dish.

"That's enough," the man said. "We don't want them getting fat. We want them to sing."

"Yes, sir."

"Singing is a great comfort, don't you agree?"

"Yes, sir."

"You may call me Maurice. Everyone does. We don't stand on ceremony. Indeed, most people find that they don't stand at all."

"Um . . ."

"Ceiling height and all."

"Ah, yes."

"That was a joke, Mr. Barlo. You may laugh if you wish."

"Thank you, sir."

"Maurice."

"Yes. Thank you, Maurice. I'm sure I'll laugh next time. You took me by surprise."

"Yes, of course." The cigar glowed briefly brighter. "But why wait? Who knows when the next opportunity will present itself?"

"Um . . ."

"Go ahead."

Even in the dimness, Hap blushed. "Ha-ha?"

"Very good! Thank you. Quite enjoyable. Moving on to practical matters, you'll find a ledge over there to put your gear. Oh," he said, "I see you don't have any. Well, then, let's get you started. *Pec!*" he barked, his voice suddenly hard.

An old Auki hop-hobbled over, his bluish complexion hidden by wrinkles and grime. His face reminded Hap of a weathered tree stump. Only his eyes were bright. Bright yellow, as Hap noticed with alarm. Nothing alarming about yellow eyes in general, of course, especially in cats. But in this creature, by torchlight, well, it was quite a different thing.

"I'd like you to meet our new recruit." Maurice gave a nod toward Hap. "We'll start Mr. Barlo on drilling the emplacements."

The old one gave an emphatic nod. "Yes, Mr. Maurice, sir."

"Mr. Slag wanted to put him on setting the charges, but I'm afraid he'd blow us all up. Can't have that, can we?"

Pec again nodded, and this time his mouth twisted up in an imitation of a smile. Aukis, Hap was learning, were not very good at smiling.

"Well, then," Maurice went on abruptly, "what are we waiting for? We've got quotas to meet."

Pec laid a bony hand on Hap's shoulder. "This way, human." His fingernails were long and hard and made Hap want to squirm free. He forced himself not to.

They started off, the boy keeping his head down to avoid low-hanging rocks. In the darkness behind them, Hap heard Maurice mutter, "You want to blow up Aukis, that's one thing, isn't it? But *I'm* down here, too!"

Hap glanced back and saw the cigar glowing in the darkness.

The Aukis had returned to work but kept casting glances at Hap. Pec seemed not to notice. With his fingernails still biting the boy's shoulder, he led the way through a side tunnel toward a room where several Aukis were busy with picks and drills.

As they approached, a wild-haired young Auki darted out, his ankle chains jangling, and spat on the ground in front of Hap's foot. He glared at the boy, then clanked away into the darkness.

Hap looked at Pec with alarm.

"Don't expect to be liked here," said the foreman. "No, don't expect that."

"Yes, but . . ." Hap shook his head. "They don't know me. How can they hate me?"

"You're a human, aren't you?"

"But . . ."

"See the chains on their ankles? Who do you think put them there? Who? I ask you."

As they trudged on, Hap couldn't help noticing that Pec had no chains on *his* ankles. Clearly, not all Aukis were treated the same.

"You speak like us!" Hap exclaimed, suddenly realizing.

"When I must. It's a bloody ugly language. Oh, ugly, ugly."

Reaching the rock face, Pec brought over an air drill. "That button starts it," he said.

Hap tried to lift the thing. It was heavy as a man.

"Into the wall there where it's marked. Into the wall. The wall!"

"Right."

Hap managed to hold the drill up and laid the bit against the stone. *I can do this,* he thought, pushing the button. The machine let out an angry scream and flung Hap violently backward, right off his feet.

"Turn it off! Turn it off!" The Auki made a grab for the drill and punched the button. His face, corrugated with wrinkles, looked fierce. "Off, I said!"

"Sorry." But no sooner had Hap spoken than he felt a searing pain burn his cheek and forehead.

"Humans!" Pec muttered, sticking his little whip back in his belt.

The pain was keen, but Hap's sense of insult was keener. "Why did you do that?"

"Why? Why? You needed it. Here. We'll start you on something easy." He picked up a bent shovel and tossed it over. "Think you can shovel these loose stones into a trough?"

Hap nodded warily.

"Then do it! Do it!"

It was better than working the drill, but it wasn't easy. The drill would scream at the rock wall, sending shards whizzing about like shrapnel. Then Hap and two Aukis would set to work shoveling the broken stones into the trough. One of them was a teenager, by the look of him—it's hard to tell with Aukis. The other was quite old, with an ancient scar on his temple. The teen, when not scowling, ignored him; but the old one's eyes sometimes crinkled with what looked like sympathy. When Hap slipped on the shale and fell hard, the old Auki silently put out his hand and helped him up.

"Thanks," said Hap, rubbing his hip. "My name's Hap."

The other nodded and resumed his work.

"What's yours?"

The old one said something—"Bane" or "Pain," Hap couldn't quite catch it—and turned away. Apparently, talking with humans was not looked well upon.

But that one kind gesture, though not repeated, got Hap through the day. A hard day it was, filled with dirty looks and brutal work. By the end of his shift, Hap was

covered with rock dust and soaked with sweat. His arms were quivering, and his back hurt so much he thought he'd never straighten up.

A distant whistle echoed through the tunnels. Then Pec lifted his own brass whistle and blew an answering blast.

"Dinner," he called out. "Put up your tools."

Hap had never heard sweeter words. Soon after, he was standing by the tracks, waiting for transport.

"How'd you like your first day?" came an echoing voice from the darkness. It was Maurice, the man in the rocking chair. He seemed not to have moved the whole time. "Pleasant work, on the whole, don't you agree?"

"Well . . ."

"Don't expect it to be this easy all the time," he continued. "You arrived late, so you had only half a day."

"That was half a day?" Hap couldn't believe he'd have to work twice as long tomorrow.

A distant grumble of metal announced that his ride was coming.

"Enjoy your evening," came the voice, accompanied by a faint clink of ice cubes.

The train ground to a stop, and Hap tumbled in.

Thirteen

DINNER WAS IN the mess hall, a drafty wooden structure filled with hard-faced men—eighty at least—sitting on benches at long tables. Each had a bowl of sour-tasting mush that a woman at the front of the room ladled out for them. A hunk of bread went with it and a cup of tea so foul-tasting Hap pushed it aside.

He looked at the others. Most were silent, thinking their own thoughts, or no thoughts at all. It's hard to think when your arms are aching so badly you can barely lift your spoon. Still, he kept glancing around, hoping to catch sight of his father.

Dad, I'm going to take you away from here.

There was no sign of him. Did he eat at a different time from the others?

And where were the Aukis? There wasn't a blue face in the room. Apparently, they didn't mix with humans, or didn't want to.

And the women? Except for the hard-eyed matron doling out food, Hap hadn't seen any women at all.

He glanced at the man at his elbow, an old fellow slurping his slop directly from the bowl, not bothering with the spoon. Hap wasn't a fancy eater, but even he flinched at the sounds the man made.

On Hap's other side sat a man who wasn't eating at all, just staring blankly ahead.

"Hello there," said Hap in a bright voice.

Slowly, the man's head turned.

"Name's Hap."

No response.

"Aren't you eating?"

The next person down leaned forward. It was a boy, maybe fifteen years old. His left eye was closed—*blind*, Hap realized—the other open and friendly. "Tomas don't talk much," he said. "He'll eat if you feed 'im. That's it."

"Oh," said Hap.

"Come on, Tom," the boy said. He spooned some mush into the man's half-open mouth. Not all of it got in.

"What happened to him?" said Hap.

"I'll tell you sometime." He spooned in another mouthful. "But not with him sittin' here. Gets him upset." He paused a beat. "You don't want to get Tomas upset."

Hap stuck out his hand. "My name's Hap."

The other, despite a blind eye and a filthy face, had an easy smile that made you want to trust him. He reached in front of Tomas and shook hands. "Name's Markie."

The two talked while Tom, between them, said nothing. It was like talking around a doorpost.

Markie was glad to answer Hap's questions about the way things worked. He'd been here several years and knew everyone. He laughed when he heard where Hap had been assigned. "Have you met Maurice yet?"

"I have."

"Watch out for him."

"Oh?"

"And watch out for the Auki they call Pec."

"I will."

"And of course, watch out for Slag."

"Anybody I shouldn't watch out for?"

"Watch out for everybody. That includes me. Slag has his spies everywhere."

Hap gave him a smiling look. "Are you a spy?"

"Would I tell you if I was?"

"Good point. So," he said, "what did you do to get sent here?"

"I didn't show proper respect. They say I made a rude noise when Ludmilla the Large came by."

"Did you?"

"Never could pass up the chance for a laugh."

Hap thought about that. He'd been tempted himself, more than once. "Sounds like an expensive laugh."

"It was," he said, "but if you're always figuring expenses, you're not going to get much laughing done." He glanced at Tomas the Doorpost. "This fella could use a few laughs himself."

"My father used to laugh a lot. He was the funniest man in Aplanap. And the best singer."

"Was?"

"He was sent here a year and a half ago."

Markie nodded. "What's the name?"

"Silas Barlo. Have you seen him?"

He rubbed his chin thoughtfully. Some of the dirt flaked off and flitted into his bowl. "Let me think about that."

Their conversation was interrupted by a loud whistle. Everyone turned to the front as Mr. Slag, dressed in military khaki and wearing his snap-brim hat, strode into the hall, with his two black dogs straining at the leash. He sprang onto the platform and held up a hand for silence, not that anyone, by now, was talking.

Hap couldn't help thinking about Grel's dog, Rauf. He wouldn't have a chance against these monsters. Then there was Sophia. They could have had her for breakfast.

Stay hidden, girl. Hap's eyes clamped shut with the force of his wish.

"Your attention, please," the commander called out. "We need to go over changes in your work schedules." He proceeded to spend several minutes going down a list of assignments. Hap didn't understand much of it. What he did understand were the sharp, dangerous angles of Slag's features and the threat in his voice.

"You'll notice," Slag said, "that these new assignments mean we'll be digging deeper than before. You'll be issued special gloves and headgear to deal with the new conditions." His eyes scanned the room like a searchlight, focusing on each face in turn. He caught Hap's eye for a moment, long enough to jerk his mouth into a smile.

"That's all for now. I wish you a good rest tonight and good work tomorrow." With that, Slag jumped from the platform, punched a fist in the air, and made for the door, the dogs thudding along beside him.

"New conditions?" murmured Hap, turning to Markie.

"Heat. Haven't you noticed, the deeper we dig, the warmer it gets?"

"I wondered about that."

"We've all been wondering. Don't make sense."

"What do you think it is?"

He shrugged. "Either we're inside a volcano or—well, you've heard the stories."

"Stories?"

"About the mountain."

"Some."

"That it's not just a mountain. It's the center of the world."

"Don't know that one."

"And at the center of it all, in the center of the center of the world, there's this blue—"

A deafening whistle blew, announcing the end of dinner. Men all around got up and carried their bowls to the back.

"There's a what?" said Hap.

"Some sort of blue stone." The whistle blew a second time. "Talk later." He got Tom the Doorpost to his feet and was guiding him to the back of the hall. Hap followed behind.

"What barracks are you bunking in?" said Markie when they were outside.

"The one up ahead, I think."

"Same as us. We'll walk you."

Hap's head was spinning with questions. A practical soul, he was usually quick to figure things out, but nothing made sense—not Maurice's ice cubes or Tomas's silence or Slag's work orders. And the Aukis, how did they fit in?

Under the questions were mysteries, and under the mysteries was the mountain itself. Holding the top of his jacket closed, Hap followed the strange pair as they scuffed along the snowy path toward the future.

PART THREE
Shadow

Fourteen

THE SPACE BEHIND the main stove was not clean, but it was warm, even after the kitchen had been shut down for the night. It was here that Sophia made her nest.

We have not forgotten about Miss Sophia—and of course, neither had Mr. Slag, who never forgot anything. He had one pink sock to go on, and he was determined to find the foot that fit into it.

Fortunately, the girl had protectors. One of the scullery women lent her a blanket, and for a pillow Sophia rolled up the fleecy coat Grel had given her. And in a kitchen that size, surrounded by supportive women, food was never a problem.

Nightmares were. The worst was one that recurred in various forms: An enormous snapping turtle, with eyes as green as Slag's, would lunge from a lake and grab hold of Hap's foot, or sometimes his hand, and start dragging him under the surface. More than once, Sophia's cries would wake up the others.

For there were two other children who slept in the kitchen. They were twins, a boy and girl, much younger than Sophia. Orphans, she'd been told. The mayor of Aplanap didn't believe in coddling unproductive citizens and had shipped them off to Xexnax. All around the prison camp, you could find the occasional child tucked away and protected. Mag the mule driver made sure of that.

But Sophia wasn't content to be tucked away. She was here to save Hap. Her problem was contacting him without being detected. Kept in the back as a kitchen helper, she had no way to mingle with miners. Often, she peeked out through the door and caught sight of her friend talking with one of the men. It bothered her to see Hap's face so dirty and his eyes so tired, but at least he was alive.

Sophia's main protector during this time was Mag's cousin Gert, the big, slab-faced woman who ladled out the mush. Gert was a tough old creature, as tough as mule-driver Mag herself, but she'd taken Sophia in without question. If Slag was after her, Gert would hide her, simple as that.

And Gert was smarter than she looked. When she'd learned that soldiers were on their way with their dogs to sniff out Sophia's hiding place, Gert had hustled the girl into an unused oven and started hammering fistfuls of garlic with a mallet. The aroma made the soldiers' noses wrinkle and the dogs' eyes water. For hours afterward, they could smell nothing but garlic.

Still, Sophia couldn't hide in the kitchen forever. Slag's speech that first night had upset her. The change in mining assignments meant more danger for everyone, including Hap. The last time she had seen him, she'd thought his face was flushed, as if he'd spent too much time near a hot stove.

She had to do something.

And then she knew what it was. That evening, finishing her chores, she went up to Gert. "I've got to find somebody," she said.

The big woman set down her dishrag. "All right," she said.

Sophia glanced around. The twins were in the corner giggling and throwing bread balls at each other. "A man named Silas Barlo."

Gert was silent.

Sophia searched her face. "Do you know him?"

"I might."

"Do you or don't you?"

"What do you want with him?"

"I don't think I can tell you." Sophia saw the way Gert looked at her and hesitated. She was going to have to trust somebody. "Maybe I *can* tell you. It's a big secret, though."

"I don't like secrets. They lead to trouble."

"This one could lead to a lot of trouble."

The woman sighed. "Well," she said, "I suppose it wouldn't be the first time."

So, in a low voice, Sophia told about Hap and his plan to rescue his father and bring him back to Aplanap.

For half a minute, Gert said nothing. "Which one is Hap?" she said at last.

"He's the boy. The younger one out there."

"I noticed him. He don't look so good to me."

"Don't say that! Mag says he's going to die like her old mule!"

"Jack is dying?"

"No, but he will one day."

Gert raised her large head to look at a corner of the ceiling. "What good will it do to talk to Barlo?"

"What good? Well, first I'd tell him about Hap. He probably doesn't know his son's here looking for him."

Gert was silent.

"Then we'd find a way to get them together."

Still no comment.

"Then the three of us will put our heads together and figure out an escape plan. Four of us, if you'll help."

Gert shook her head.

"What?" said Sophia.

"You don't have a plan. You have a hope. There's no room for hope on this mountain."

"You mean you won't help?"

"I don't think so."

The girl stared at her. You could see the anger building. "Then who will?"

"Nobody with any sense."

"*Somebody* must know where Silas Barlo is."

"Sure. Mr. Slag knows. Why don't you ask him?"

"You're making fun of me."

"I'm trying to keep you alive."

"You don't understand," Sophia said slowly. "If I want to save Hap, I'm going to have to save his dad, because Hap won't leave without him."

Gert sat down heavily and pulled over a plate of nut cookies. "Wish I could help."

"Who can?"

"Have a cookie."

"Who *can?*"

"Aside from Slag, I don't know. He's got it all in his ledger book."

"Where does he keep this book?"

"Don't even think about it."

"*Where?*"

"In his hands. He's never without it." Gert saw the look on her face. "*You can't get it.*"

"I'll find a way."

"You stay where you are."

"But I'm no use to anybody!"

"You're of use to me. And your friend out there would be happy knowing you're safe."

"He'd be happier knowing where his father is."

Gert wasn't listening. She was gathering greasy rags in a pile to be washed.

Sophia watched her moving about the kitchen. *Look at her. I bet she knows exactly where Silas Barlo is.*

Gert hung a heavy pot on its hook. "What are you thinking about over there?" she said.

I'll find a way. He's got to put that ledger down sometime.

Sophia smiled. "I was wondering if I could have some more of these cookies."

Fifteen

Sophia was right to worry about her friend. As the days wore on, Hap became both harder and softer. His hands were callused, and he could sling rocks around like an Auki, but the heat at the lower levels where he worked was intense, and he often felt dizzy as he dragged himself into the mess hall at night.

"You're Hap, right?"

He looked up into the round, red face of the woman known as Gert. He'd seen her often enough, but she'd never spoken to him before.

"That's right," he said.

"We've got a problem." She ladled greasy mush into his bowl and handed him a hunk of bread. "She's disappeared."

"Who?"

"Your friend."

"You mean . . ." He looked around. "You mean Sophia?"

"Come back for seconds. We'll talk."

In a daze, Hap carried his tray to the table. His friend Markie glanced up. "You all right?" he said through a mouthful of bread.

"Guess so."

Sophia! He'd finally found out where she'd been, only to learn she was gone. He wolfed his food and headed to the front of the hall.

"I think," said Gert, glancing around for spies, "she's trying to find your father."

"That's way too dangerous!"

The woman shushed him with a look. "It's worse," she murmured. "She may be trying to get a peek at Slag's ledger book—the one he always has with him?"

He nodded. "I remember it."

"I don't know. Maybe I shouldn't of told you."

"No, no, you did the right thing."

"Slag's not someone to fool around with."

"I won't."

"I mean it." She filled his bowl. "I'm talking to a wall, aren't I?"

Hap smiled.

Slowly, he walked back to the table. Markie looked up, his good eye bright and questioning. He'd been trying to get Tomas to chew a hunk of bread.

"Where does Mr. Slag sleep?" Hap said.

"In the headquarters building. Why?"

"Just curious."

Markie gave him an odd look. "Any time."

Hap's own sleeping quarters were in a building not far from the mess hall. The beds were actually shelves, with thin mattresses and thinner blankets. There were heat pipes, as in the headquarters building, but only one to a floor. They barely warmed the bedrooms.

Hap climbed to his bunk. Soon others arrived, played a game or two of Plog, and tucked in early. They had to, given the five a.m. wake-up and ten-hour day. Hap lay listening. Should he have told Markie what he'd learned? He liked the kid but didn't know how far to trust him. As open as Markie could be talking about himself and how he'd lost his eye (a shard of rock flung from an air drill), he was cagey and evasive when asked about Silas.

Everybody seems to know something, and nobody will tell me anything.

When the men were snoring, Hap climbed down, picked up his shoes and coat, and slipped into the hall. He'd been thinking about Sophia, about where she might go if she really wanted to get a look at Slag's ledger book. He decided to scout out the headquarters first.

Although Hap knew Slag had many spies, there were few guards, and in the barracks, there was only an elderly night watchman. After all, where would anyone run? Howling wind and driving snow did not inspire schemes of escape.

The corridor was lit by a kerosene lamp. Beneath it

gently snored the watchman, a copy of the *Daily Aplanapian* spread out over his paunch. The door was just beyond.

Shoes in hand, Hap sidled along the hall. He realized he had to step over the watchman's outstretched legs. *Whatever you're dreaming about*, he thought, *keep dreaming*. The splintery floor gave a sad creak as Hap lifted his foot. He froze. No reaction. He stepped over.

As he did, he noticed part of a headline:

BLUE S

The rest was hidden in a fold of the paper. With painful care, Hap lifted the top page. Suddenly, the whole newspaper cascaded to the floor. The old man's eyes fluttered, as if deciding between waking and sleep. Then they closed again. Seconds later, Hap was outside.

He scanned the paper while he tied his laces.

BLUE SHOE TO CLOSE

A cobbler's shop that gained fame throughout the three-mountain region is slated to close next week, after its primary attraction, a remarkable gem-encrusted shoe, lost its brilliance and failed to perform as expected.

The Blue Shoe, as the shop is known, has been operated for many years by a cobbler who gave his name as Grel. Until recently, it was the most popular establishment in Aplanap, attracting the curious from as far away as . . .

Hap glanced at the top of the page. This was last week's paper! The shop had probably closed already. Grel and Rauf would be out on the street.

Before long, they'd be begging!

Hap shoved his fists in his pockets and set out briskly in the direction of headquarters, the crusted snow crunching under his shoes. He was going to rescue Sophia, and he was going to rescue his father, and he would have to be quick about it. Grel was in danger.

Sixteen

GREL WAS INDEED in danger, but then so were many citizens of Aplanap. You remember the bustling shops, warm breezes, and bright flower boxes of a few weeks ago. Well, now instead of tourists, solitary souls huddled in doorways, collars turned up against a gritty wind. Trash sat in sad piles by the curb, with no one to collect it. The curiosity shop remained open, just barely, with Sophia's parents reducing prices and then reducing them again. The cuckoo clock makers fared worse, and the jewelers worst of all. Who but Ludmilla the Large could afford rings and necklaces? And she never paid.

Weather was blamed for the town's sudden decline. In the weeks since Hap's departure, the wind had sharpened and spun around from new angles, whipping up great swaths of sand from the shore of Doubtful Bay and swirling them high over Aplanap. Citizens stayed indoors to avoid getting sand in their eyes and down the back of their necks. It goes without saying the quince crop was ruined.

At last, after two days, the sun came out, and people began sweeping the sand from their stoops and scooping it out of their geranium boxes. They shook their heads in wonder at the strange weather they'd had. Some even made jokes about it.

The more superstitious, poking their noses out the door and sniffing the air, blamed everything on the blue shoe. Especially, they blamed that little sneak thief Hap Barlo—no better than his father—who had stolen a gem from the shoe's heel. What could you expect after that except bad weather and fat ravens circling the trash piles? And beggars! Yes, there were now beggars in Aplanap, with no one to arrest them. There seemed no point. If you arrested two, three more appeared in their place.

The following week, when the weather was fading as a topic of conversation, the thermometer suddenly dipped and the winds again turned angry. The citizens were angry, too. After all, one expected unpleasantness on Mount Xexnax, to the north, but not in fair Aplanap, which had always been protected by the taller peaks around it. The temperature fell and fell, no apologies, and the winds switched around eleven ways before dinner. A blizzard of sand zigzagged through town.

This time it was worse than before. When the storm ended, at midnight a day and a half later, the town was buried up to its doorknobs.

Jon Hartpence, Sophia's brother, had been kept awake that night by the wind. Suddenly, he didn't hear it anymore. It was as if someone had reached out and switched it off. Puzzled, he went to the window. Down the block, the banners hung lifeless from the towers of the Town Hall—no hint of a breeze anywhere. Overhead, a brilliant moon laid silver over the sand-filled streets. Never had the world been so quiet.

Jon was about to turn back to bed when he noticed a short, dark figure limping through the swollen dunes covering the sidewalk.

Who would be out at this time of night? A beggar, no doubt, but who was there to beg from? A ratty blanket covered the poor fellow's head and trailed along behind, leaving a glimmering track, like a snail's. A trick of moonlight, no doubt.

Go home, old man, Jon thought. *This is not a night to be out.*

The creature hobbled on, leaning heavily on a short crutch, while behind him the mysterious trail of silver began to spread, like midnight water in a boat's wake.

The moon stared down with single-eyed intensity.

The beggar disappeared.

Next morning, the sun rose clear and sharp. People looked out in astonishment. Never had anyone seen such blinding beauty! They'd been expecting sand. Instead, all the houses, gardens, and streets shone like the inside of a diamond. There was no diamond, of course, much to Ludmilla's disappointment, but clearly, something hard, smooth, and brilliant had coated everything in sight—indeed, welded it in place.

The mayor immediately sent out forecasters, geologists, astronomers, and anyone with an opinion to examine the strange substance. They tapped it, magnified it, subjected it to caustic chemicals. At length, they came together to discuss their findings. They tugged thoughtfully on their beards, then nodded and tugged their beards some more. This went on most of the afternoon. Finally, they delivered their verdict: The town of Aplanap was encased in glass.

Impossible! It had to be ice of some sort. And yet, as the temperature rose from cold to cool, and from cool to faintly warm, there was no sign of melting. Sparkling glassicles bearded the postboxes. Trees wore elaborate necklaces, each twig so slick that birds slipped off as soon as they tried to alight. There were even several beggars found crouched against buildings, their cups extended. They had turned into exhibits of beggars. Glassed-in exhibits.

Many theories were offered. The most frequently heard was that silica in the blowing sand had fused in the atmosphere and returned to earth in the form of glass. But the common people stuck to a simpler explanation: It was magic. Bad magic.

Many prayers were said that day, even a few to the goddess Xexnax, in whom no one had believed for nine hundred years.

The children of Aplanap paid no attention to all this. They were delighted and raced outside, only to find themselves sliding helplessly down the street, unable to stop. The old games, like tag, weren't possible, because no one could stand up long enough to play them. No matter. The air soon filled with sounds of hilarity as new games were invented, like Slide and Sneak.

Rag, the youngest son of quince-pickers, did not join in. Life for him had turned serious ever since he'd glanced outside and seen that his pet goat—the family's only source of milk—had turned to glass in the front yard. Indeed, for many poor families, food of any sort was hard to find.

Ordinary life came to a standstill. Postmen couldn't get up the tilted streets to deliver mail. Firewood couldn't be had for the bakers' ovens. The sick slid right past the hospital. Even the tax collectors found it impossible to make their rounds.

Ludmilla was furious. Like others, she blamed Hap Barlo for the town's troubles. "Why didn't we hang the boy when we had the chance?" she fumed. "Give those ravens something to peck at!"

"Now, now, dear," said the mayor with the endless name. "We did what we could. We sent him to his death, didn't we?"

"He got off easy," she humphed.

The mayor could see the sweat lines in the creases of her neck, a sign that his wife was in a dangerous mood. "We should look on the bright side," he said, attempting a smile. "The news from Mr. Slag is good."

"You believe that thug?"

"We hired him."

"Right out of prison."

"He has yet to disappoint us. And he says he's located the gem. The surveyor has pinpointed it."

"I'll believe that," replied the mountainous woman, "when I am holding it in my hand."

"It might take *two* hands. That's what the legend says."

His wife's tiny eyes brightened in spite of her. "You think so?"

"That's what they say. Of course, there are all kinds of legends. For instance, whoever owns it lives forever."

"I could get used to that."

"You'd have a long time to get used to it. You'd also know everything."

"Would I really?"

"Everything in the world."

"All right. But about the jewel—is it very bright?"

"Blinding."

"And is it really blue?"

"As the summer sky."

Ludmilla's face settled into folds of greed. So the Xexnax diamond, known as the Great Blue, was not just a story after all. Modern measurements had calculated its exact location in the heart of that heartless mountain. Within days, it would be hers!

Her lips twisted into a wormy smile. "You're sure it's not made of glass?"

"Pure diamond."

The smile widened.

Her husband beamed at her.

"Come here, you naughty boy," she purred, lowering her eyelids demurely. "Give your Luddy a kiss."

At the other end of town from the mayor's mansion stood the curio shop, Xexnax Knickknacks. There was no kissing going on there. Even the house had an unkissed look. After all, when you're constantly fighting, you're much too busy to fix a sagging door or replace a window.

Jon and Sophia's parents quarreled all the time. They quarreled about whether Mrs. Hartpence's tea was hot enough or whether Mr. Hartpence's cocoa was cool enough. They disagreed about what to charge for souvenir mugs and whether to lower their prices again and where to place the racks of picture postcards.

One evening at dinner, some weeks after their daughter's disappearance, they were discussing whether or not to change the shop's doorbell from *ding-ding* to the more authoritative *ding-dong* when Mrs. Hartpence chanced to look up and notice that a chair was empty.

"Where's Sophia?"

Jon looked up from his boiled cabbage. "You mean you just noticed *now*?"

"Noticed what?"

"Sophia's gone."

"Impossible! I just saw her . . ." Her voice trailed off. "When was it?"

Sophia's father frowned. "It couldn't have been more than . . ."

"Father," said Jon, "she's been gone for weeks!"

"What!" cried the woman. "Poor baby! What happened?"

Jon's headache was kicking up again. He massaged his skull with his fingers. "I helped her sneak into the prison. I showed her where the air ducts were, and she crawled inside. Do you have any of that headache tea left?"

"You helped her *what?*" cried Mother. "Why?"

"She wanted to save Hap."

"Hap's in prison?"

"He was." Jon massaged his skull harder than before. "You didn't *know* that? Everybody knew that!"

"Nobody tells us anything. Do you think she's still in there?"

"In prison? No. I crawled in the next day looking for her. Nothing but dust and mouse droppings."

"Why didn't you *say* something?" demanded Mrs. Hartpence.

"I couldn't get your attention."

"That's silly! I always want to know what my children are doing."

Jon was so amazed by this he didn't know what to say. His head had begun to throb.

"Well," said Jon's father, "*I* certainly care. You could have told *me!*"

"Are you saying," said the woman, "that you care more than I do?"

"Isn't it obvious?"

"It certainly is not. Quite the opposite!"

"That's outrageous!"

"Admit it. You never cared about your children."

"Untrue!"

"True!"

Neither of them noticed that their son had quietly gotten up from his chair and left the room.

The wooden pieces clacked on the little table outside the cobbler's shop. Grel's concentration was off, and besides, the table was coated in glass. With the slightest breeze, the pieces slid to the ground.

"Come on, old man, try again," said his friend the watchmaker after beating Grel a third time.

"It's no use." Grel looked down at Rauf. The dog's tail waved feebly. "It's bad enough I don't have food for myself, but Rauf—look at his ribs!"

"Dogs will always find scraps," said the watchmaker. But he didn't sound convinced. *People* were eating scraps these days.

Grel took his pipe out of his mouth and stared into its empty bowl. Who had money for tobacco?

"At least you still have customers," said his friend.

"True." Grel tapped his chin thoughtfully with the

pipestem. He didn't need to add that very few of these customers paid him. The shop, in fact, was officially closed. He was allowed to stay on because of one very important customer: Ludmilla the Large, a woman whose fascination with footwear nearly equaled her desire for diamonds.

She was an expensive customer to have. She demanded the softest leathers and finest buckles but was not obliged to pay for them. The arrangement was supposed to save Hap, but it had not saved Hap, and it was ruining Grel.

"Come on," said the watchmaker, setting up the board. "Another game of Plog."

The game had scarcely begun when they spied a boy struggling up the slick street in their direction. For a breath-catching moment, Grel thought it was Hap coming home at last, but then he realized this boy was taller. In fact, it was the mayor's nephew, the same snide seventeen-year-old who long ago had tried to steal the blue shoe. There was no danger he'd want to steal it now.

The boy fell hard, then grabbed on to a glass-coated streetlamp and fell again. Finally, bruised and out of breath, he arrived at the shop.

"Good afternoon," said Grel.

"Likely story," said the youngster.

"What brings you to see us?"

"What do you think? Aunt Ludmilla's shoes, of course. The last pair was totally unacceptable."

"I'm sorry to hear it."

"Sorry my eye!"

"I did my best," he answered truthfully.

131

"Your best! Did Auntie ask for gold buckles or not?"

"She did."

"You gave her brass. Brass!"

"I had no gold."

"Well, you were to *get* it!"

"Brass was hard enough to get."

The boy drew himself up. "In other words," he said, "you have broken the agreement."

"I suppose that's true."

"And you intend to continue breaking your agreement in the future."

"Well, if she requires gold . . ."

"In that case . . ." The boy took out a roll of parchment, somewhat wrinkled from his several falls on the way over. "In that case," he said again, and cleared his throat, "I am instructed to deliver this notice of eviction." He handed the document to Grel, who passed it to the watchmaker.

"You read it," said the cobbler.

The watchmaker unrolled the notice. " 'It having been established that Grel the cobbler, known as the Party of the First Part . . .' "

"Yes, yes. Skip to the bottom."

"It says you need to get out by noon tomorrow."

"Noon tomorrow," repeated Grel.

"That's right!" crowed the mayor's nephew. "So you'd better get cracking, old man!"

Grel ignored him. "Well," he said, patting Rauf's head, "that's that. Shall we finish our game of Plog?"

Seventeen

I MUST TAKE a moment and apologize to young Hap
Barlo, who deserves better treatment. Blame it on that
newspaper article, which sent us back to Aplanap and all
that was happening there. As a result, poor Hap was left
standing in the snow at midnight with inadequate shoes.

Midnight on Mount Xexnax is not pleasant in the
best of shoes. To make matters worse, Hap wasn't at all
sure which way to go. There were half a dozen buildings
in sight, all of them dark, with only an occasional lamp in
an occasional window. With freezing hands rubbing his
stinging ears, Hap came to a fieldstone house with a
porch and a flight of wooden steps. Yes, there above the
door were the carved letters XCC. He scanned the building, trying to figure the best way in.

The breath suddenly caught in his throat. He thought he'd seen a movement under the staircase, a shadow among shadows. It could have been a trick of the moon, which had just emerged from a cloud and was flooding the snow with ghostly light.

There it was again.

A figure emerged from under the steps. He was beckoning.

With nowhere to hide, Hap decided to go forward.

"Quick!" the stranger called in a whisper. "Out of the light!"

Hap stepped into the building's shadow.

"Thought you'd come," said the other. He seemed to be winking, but then Hap saw that his left eye was permanently closed.

"Markie!"

"Shh."

"What are you doing here?"

"Stopping you."

Hap was stunned. "But how did you—?"

"No questions. The building's protected all kinds of ways. Your friend didn't know that."

"My friend?"

"She climbed in a window last night and got caught."

Hap was about to speak, but Markie stopped him. "Come," he said. He followed the line of the house to the edge, then crept along the side, always keeping to the shadows.

At the rear of the building, behind a brake of scrubby trees, a path led off into the darkness.

"Wait," said Hap. "Where are you *going?* We've got to rescue Sophia."

"Not now. Stay with me."

The trail led generally upward before petering out among icy crags. Markie shook his head, seeing Hap struggle. "You sure picked the wrong shoes for rock climbing."

"Don't remind me."

Hap peered ahead but despite the moonlight could see nothing but stone and ice, with stunted evergreens between. Another stretch and they reached a wide ledge, where Hap noticed packed-down snow and a long crack in the rock face. Getting nearer, he saw that the opening was wide enough to step through, and it led inside the mountain.

Markie went first, lighting a kerosene lamp that hung inside the entrance. "They got here before us," he said quietly.

"Who?"

"Watch your step."

It was warmer within. The stones were wet with ice melt and slippery with lichen as the friends made their way. Hap was surprised to see an orange glow ahead. Uncertain at first, it grew brighter as they went on. Finally, turning a corner and ducking beneath stalactites, they stepped into a high, open area, wide as a train station. In the center, half a dozen people stood beside a fire.

They were all looking at Hap.

He looked at them as well but had trouble making out faces silhouetted against the flames.

One of the men moved aside, and a dwarfish creature stepped forward. Hap realized at once it was an Auki—one he'd seen before. It took a moment to place him, but the woolen watch cap and tufted eyebrows gave him away.

"What," exclaimed Hap, "are *you* doing here?"

"Welcomen, sone," said Ulf, the ferryboat captain. "We been expecting ye."

As Hap stepped closer, other faces revealed themselves amid the dancing shadows. He didn't recognize the men, but there among them, bigger than anyone, stood Mag the mule driver.

"Well, well," she said.

"Hello, Mag," said Hap.

"Here's a mug of tea to warm your gizzards."

Hap took the drink gratefully. The steam, with the mingled scents of cinnamon and clove, tingled against his face.

"We hear your friend's got herself in a bit of trouble," she said.

Ulf cleared his throat. "Shouldst ye nought ha brought her in the first place, but let that pass."

Markie spoke up, introducing the others. Most were miners, but one—a tall, somber-faced man in military khakis—was a guard. "These are your friends," said Markie. "Learn their faces."

Hap looked around at them. "My friends?"

"The underground. The resistance," Markie supplied. "Ulf here is our leader."

Hap was confused. Ulf hadn't seemed the smartest creature he'd ever met. Then he remembered Mag's words: *Sometimes it's smart to be dumb.* It might have been Ulf who'd taught her that.

"We figured," said Markie, "since we're all in the same game, it would be good to know who's playing on your side."

"What game is that?"

"That's what we call it, in case we're overheard by the wrong ears."

"I see. And the game is . . . ?"

"Revolt."

"Freedom," said Ulf.

"Doom to evildoers," said Mag, crossing her arms before her.

Hap had to smile. "And you expect to go up against Slag and his guns?"

"There's more of us than you see, but you don't need to know 'em," said Markie. "Better you don't."

Hap sipped carefully from the mug. "How do you know you can trust me?"

"A fair question. For one thing, we've been watching you. And then . . ." He looked around at the others. Ulf nodded. "And then," Markie went on, "your dad said you were all right."

"My *father!*" Hap's heart started beating hard. "You know where he is?"

"We do. He's been sending us messages."

"Where *is* he?"

Markie hesitated. "He's with Slag's men."

"No!" Hap burst out. "He would never—" He looked around angrily. "You don't know my dad if you think—"

"What I *meant*," said Markie, "is that he's *with* them. He's not one of them."

The words sank in. "That sounds dangerous."

"It is."

"Is he . . ." Hap could hardly say it. "Is he all right?"

Everyone was silent.

"Will somebody say something?"

Mag put a weighty arm around Hap's shoulder. "He's a brave man," she said. "Brave as my Ulf."

"Here," said Markie, "maybe you should have a seat." He sat down near the fire and patted the stone beside him. "We've got a lot to go over."

For the next twenty minutes, Markie and the others told the boy what they knew. When he'd arrived on the mountain, Silas had been as miserable as anyone could be. He was known among his co-workers as "the silent one." Finally, he got so bad it was either die or—sing.

"Your dad has quite a voice," said the man in the guard's uniform.

"I know," said Hap.

"Singing," said Markie quietly, "was his way of not dying."

Hap bit his underlip. It hurt to think of his father this way.

"Anyway, it made him feel better," Markie went on. "Made others feel better, too."

Hap nodded.

"The guards didn't know what to do. There's no actual regulation against singing in the mine, since nobody'd done it before; but it's understood the workers aren't there to enjoy themselves. Your father was not showing the proper amount of misery."

The guards, said Markie, reported Hap's father to the foreman, and the foreman reported him to the overseer. Finally, he was brought before Slag himself, who ordered him separated from the others and kept in headquarters to entertain Slag's men exclusively.

That was how the former beekeeper from Aplanap ended up in the inner circle of Xexnax Command Central. It was only a small step to becoming a spy.

"He doesn't know about you yet," Markie added.

"But you said—"

"He talks about you all the time. Says how trustworthy you are. But he has no idea you're here."

"You've got to tell him!"

Markie stroked his chin. "We're afraid how it might affect him. We don't want to throw him off. He's too useful."

"Useful!"

"Yes. Except for him, we wouldn't know your friend's been captured or where she's held. I call that useful."

Hap couldn't argue. "So, where are they holding her?"

"There are cells in the basement of the headquarters building."

"We've got to get her out of there!"

"We will," said Markie. "Soon as we can figure out how."

"What do they want with her?"

"They're asking her questions."

"Interrogating her?"

No one spoke. Big Mag came over and sat beside Hap. "We all want to rescue her, and your dad, of course." She glanced over at Ulf. "But there's more than them involved. There's a whole *mountain* of people."

Hap was staring into the fire.

"Slag's after something," Mag went on. "Your father's learning what he can. So, you see, we don't want to rescue him too soon."

Hap looked from Mag to Ulf.

"He nic *want* it," said the Auki, "ere he leornst hwaet Slag's aboot."

Hap recalled that he himself had once told somebody not to rescue him. "But Sophia—"

"Different story," said Markie. "But tricky."

Hap remembered how Sophia had once crawled through the air vents of the Aplanap prison to save him. "I'll do anything," he said.

"We know you will," said Mag.

"Meanwhile," said Markie, "you might want to hold on to this." He handed the boy a tattered little book. "I found this in the snow outside the window of the head-quarters."

Hap stared down at it. *One Hundred Easy Spells for Beginners*.

He slipped the book in his pocket.

Eighteen

THE SMOKE WAS so thick the soldiers could barely make out the face of the man standing on the table, and their voices were so loud they could hardly hear him sing.

It was a sweet song, a little sad, about life in old Aplanap. For the older soldiers, those who remembered happier days, it was a favorite.

And Silas knew how to keep a song fresh. Every time he sang "The Cuckoos of Aplanap," the words were a little different, as if he were making them up on the spot. The soldiers liked that, too.

"So clever he is," remarked a bewhiskered gent, giving his head a shake.

"Another round, boy!" yelled an impatient guardsman at the end, thumping his tankard on the table.

The serving boy, a tall, resentful-looking lad on the fringe of his first mustache, set down the tray he was carrying and wiped his hands on his pants bottom. "Hold on, I'll get to you. Gert's just bringing in a new barrel."

"You hear that? He'll get to you," called out another, leaning back and clunking a booted foot on the table. "In his good time."

"Silence!" A sharp, clear voice rang out. Mr. Slag had entered the room, with his black dogs on a leash and his short shotgun jammed in his belt. He tossed his hat on the table. "I want to hear this fellow Silas."

Talk dwindled to a murmur as the dogs curled at their master's feet. The serving boy came around with a jug.

"Sing us something else, Mr. Barlo," said Slag. "Your songs are too sad."

"What would you like?" Silas's button-brown eyes blinked patiently, but his crooked nose gave a twitch, a sign of nerves.

"Something lively, for heaven's sake." Slag squinted at him through the tobacco haze. "What do you know that's lively?"

"There's that hiking song I used to sing with my boy during our jaunts."

"That's right. You've got a son, haven't you?"

"I do."

"A fine-looking boy, for a thief."

"Excuse me?" The nose twitched, first right, then left, like a trapped hamster.

"What? You didn't know?"

Silas suddenly had trouble speaking. "Are you, um, talking about Hap Barlo?"

"That's the name. He's been our guest on the mountain for the past several weeks."

Silas couldn't speak at all.

Hap on Mount Xexnax!

"So, then," said Slag heartily, "what have you got for us? I'll tell you what. Sing us about that nose of yours. With all this smoke, it's the only part of you I can see."

A general laugh went up, followed by much quaffing of grog. Soon empty tankards were thumping on the table.

"And give us a dance while you're about it," Slag added.

"A dance and a song. Yes, sir."

145

Silas paused. It was a longer pause than usual, as if he were looking around for his voice. A soldier called out for him to hurry. Suddenly, Silas gave a slap to the little drum tucked under his arm and thrust his face forward, accentuating his crooked nose. He did a fancy shuffle and turned right around, stopping like a statue where he'd been before. "My *nose*," he sang in a rising tenor, "*my beautiful, shining nose . . .*"

A roar of laughter filled the low-ceilinged room.

Whappity-whappity-whappity on the little drum. Several men started clapping to the rhythm.

My nose is excellent at smelling.
In fact, it's smelling like a rose!
Whap-whappity!

It sniffs out crime, it sniffs out dirt,
it sniffs that fellow's undershirt.

The guard with the soiled shirt blushed red as his companions howled.

"A fine thrust, Mr. Barlo!" called Slag. "Keep on."

It smells the grog the guardsmen quaff—

Loud laughter from the two guardsmen at the table.

and smells the burp in their belly laugh.

Now everyone laughed except the guardsmen.

"Again," cried Slag, raising his mug. He glanced around at the others. "He hits again!"

But the smell that makes these nostrils
gag,
worse than the feet of an unwashed
hag . . .

The drum grew louder and Silas's voice more intense as it wound around the strange melody he was improvising.

. . . or rotten fish in a saddlebag,
or the smell of blood on a battle flag . . .

Silas did a neat pirouette and came to a stop directly facing Slag. The room fell silent. The two men stared at each other.

Whappity-whap!

. . . is the smell of a lie and the smell of a
brag
by some scurvy-minded scallywag. . . .

"Careful, Mr. Barlo," Slag breathed. One of the dogs grumbled.

But such foul thoughts need never *nag,*
no, never, never, never nag
our dear, illustrious . . .

Here Silas broke into a twinkling smile.

. . . Mr. Slag!

The room remained silent until, slowly, Slag lifted his hands and clapped them together. Then everyone clapped. More than that, they yelled with pleasure.

"Very good, Barlo," Slag said when the applause had died down. "You've earned your dinner. Why don't you take it in the kitchen?"

Silas made a short bow and climbed from the table. On his way out, he accepted slaps on the shoulder from several of the men and a wink from another.

He lurched into the kitchen, looking around distractedly. He gave a nod to Gert, who was just leaving.

"Playing it pretty close to the edge, aren't ya?" murmured the under-cook when the door had closed. He was a wooden-faced man seldom given to speech.

Silas didn't answer. He leaned his back against the wall, then slid down till he was sitting.

"Look!" said the scullery maid's little daughter. She was peeking out from the safety of her mother's skirt. "Look, Maman, he's crying! He's crying all over his funny nose."

147

Nineteen

Sᴏᴘʜɪᴀ, Hᴀᴘ ᴛʜᴏᴜɢʜᴛ, his mind taking on the rhythm of the train car rattling through the darkness. *Sophia, Sophia, Sophia* . . .

He took out Sophia's little book of spells and flipped through it. Several of the sections had her check marks next to them, and one was completely underlined: the "Never-Fail Love Spell."

Why was that particular spell so important?

The thought struck him: Was she trying to use it on *him*?

Did she really think about him that way?

For heaven's sake, he thought, this was a booklet for tourists interested in that moldy old legend! It was about as real as the little ceramic figurines of the goddess, in three sizes, that lined the store's counter. Surely she understood that!

The train arrived at the new workstation, deeper in the mountain than before. The work was hotter than yesterday, and yesterday had been hotter than the day before. Mining operations in Xexnax had definitely taken a turn: in direction, down; in temperature, up.

Hap hadn't slept much after last night's adventure and had to be extra-careful not to make mistakes, especially here, where a miscalculation could cost you an eye or an arm. To his surprise, he noticed the Aukis making blunders themselves. They lived in this mountain and knew better than that. Now they could be found digging in places they shouldn't be and not digging in places they should.

Pec, the Auki foreman, shouted at them. Sometimes he stung them with the little whip he carried in his waistband, but still they kept getting things wrong. Hap began to wonder if they were making mistakes on purpose.

But why? What did it matter where they dug? Stone was stone.

He looked from one worker to the next, gauging whether he could trust any of them. His task, Markie had told him, was to get the Aukis to help the resistance. Hap had asked the obvious question: Why not have Ulf talk to his fellow Aukis?

Ulf had looked at him with a sadness Hap hadn't seen before. No one, he said, would talk to him. They considered him a traitor for marrying a human. Now he was an outcast in both worlds, doomed to steer the ferry-boat back and forth between them.

No, Ulf had said, if anyone could win the Aukis over, it would have to be Hap.

Having a few minutes free while the shovel crew worked, Hap decided to go looking for the Auki called Baen. He was the bony old fellow with the sympathetic eyes who'd helped Hap get to his feet that awful first day in the mine. Over the weeks, they'd become almost friends. If anyone would help him, he'd be the one.

They called him Baen, or Baen Hus, but that was just a nickname, of course. No one would *actually* be named Baen Hus ("Bone House" in Auki). They called him that because he was so skinny.

Hap was the sort who made friends easily, and the others no longer spat at him. It helped that Baen, a re-spected elder, had befriended him. But what surprised the workers most was Hap's mastery of a number of Auki words. They didn't know what to make of it. He was, after all, a member of the oppressor race. Nobody like him had ever bothered to learn their language.

He set off now at a trot. Baen, he'd been told, was set-ting explosive charges in a small side tunnel not far away.

"Thaer ye erest, Baen!" Hap called out in Auki, see-ing the old fellow up ahead.

"*Habbst kear!*" cried the Auki, waving him back.

The warning to be careful came just a moment too

late. A deafening explosion knocked the boy off his feet. He blacked out, felt himself floating, then falling, all in slow motion.

Am I dead? he thought dreamily. People he knew drifted into his vision: Grel looking up from his work-bench, Silas holding out his arms, Sophia shaking her head and smiling.

A moment later, his body slammed onto the rocks, and he was shocked awake. Shocked, too, at the pain shooting up his side. Coming to his bruised senses, he cringed as dust and jagged shards from the roof rained down on him. He choked violently, as more and more de-bris fell onto him. Clawing about, he struggled desper-ately for air, but the rubble was now over his head.

Don't panic! he commanded, feeling a growing hysteria. *Can't breathe!*

Strangely, he discovered that one of his legs was free. It made no sense, unless . . . unless there was an open space *below* him!

Squirming both feet around, he dislodged some of the debris. Then, in a rush, it all fell away, and he fell with it, landing with a painful thump ten feet below, in darkness.

He gasped, taking in dusty air, coughing, choking, but breathing!

For several seconds, he was able to comprehend only one fact: He was alive—and that made him laugh despite the pain.

Then came a second realization: Wherever he was, he was too far down to climb out.

And a third: There was someone beside him! He heard a moan and, feeling around in the dark, brushed against a foot.

"Baen?"

No sound but the trickle of dirt sifting into the hole.

"Ist du, Baen?" Hap repeated. "Andsware."

"Ay, sone," came the tremulous response, followed by coughing.

Hap dug with his hands, clearing rocks and dirt, till he was able to pull his friend free. But the old Auki didn't move.

"Hwaet ist?" said Hap anxiously.

"Eom dead mon," came the faint reply.

"No! Nalas treow!"

Hap could say as much as he wanted that it was "not at all true," but it could very well be true. He'd almost died himself.

"Com, freond," he urged, but there was no reply.

"We're getting out of here," said Hap, reverting to his own language. "They'll come for us soon." It was a reasonable hope. Others were working in nearby tunnels, and they would certainly have heard the explosion.

No one came. Fifteen minutes went by, then twenty. Had the blast blocked the entrance?

Hap looked around. Apparently, they were in an abandoned tunnel of some sort, below the area currently being mined. The mountain was riddled with such excavations, and the danger of an accidental collapse was always great.

Hap decided to see where the tunnel led. Up and out, he hoped.

The first direction it took was down.

"Let's go, friend," he said. Baen was heavier than he'd expected, but Hap managed, gasping and straining, to hoist him onto his shoulder. He staggered forward.

The darkness, deep at first, became almost total. He struggled on, telling himself the tunnel had to lead somewhere. Not seeing where he was going, he stumbled face-first into a sticky net, several feet across. "Ach!" he cried, pulling the web aside. He hoped its owner wasn't around.

Then he heard a vague whispery sound, like hundreds of little feet scampering, and he shuddered. The tunnel might have been abandoned by the Aukis, but it had not been abandoned by the rats!

He felt them pattering over his shoes, flittering on all sides. He even felt small, sharp pulls on his laces. *There can't be much to eat down here,* Hap thought. *My shoes might make a meal for them.*

My feet might make a meal for them!

He pushed on, kicking and scuffing his way along. Sometimes he'd hear a squeal as his shoe connected with a rodent. Several times he stepped on something soft that gave way with a sickening squish.

"We're going to make it, Baen!" he shouted, hoping to scare the rats. They did pause briefly, as if to listen to the echo of his voice ricocheting from one end of the tunnel to the other; but then they were jumping about again, more excited than ever.

To give himself courage, Hap broke into a song, one his father used to sing in happier days, when they'd tramped together through Xexnax Park.

Happy we are a-wandering . . .

His voice was cracking.

It's what we care for most.
For just because we're wandering,
it does not mean we're lost.

No sound of scampering. The rats had probably never heard singing before. Hap hiked the old Auki higher on his shoulder and sang the next verse and the next, then started over, till his voice was hoarse.

He could see nothing. The only sound was the slow shuffle of his feet along loose stones. His side still hurt from his fall, and his back was aching. How much longer could he keep stooping over in this low tunnel? And with Baen on his back!

But he couldn't set him down. The rats would be on him in seconds!

"Are you all right?"

No answer.

Hap was at the last stage of exhaustion. It wouldn't be long now before his strength gave out completely. He paused, sweating. It was warm in here. Hot, even. Perhaps if he rested just a few minutes . . .

If you stop, you will die, said a voice in his head quite calmly. It didn't sound like his own voice, but he trusted it. He stumbled on.

Soon a strange dizziness took hold of him. In the tunnel's blackness, he imagined a blue object floating up ahead somewhere. He knew it wasn't real, but he made his way toward it. The closer he got, the more it receded.

Hap shook his head, clamped his eyes shut, then opened them.

The blue object hung in the darkness, steady as a lantern. In its vague light, he saw another tunnel forking to the right.

Which way?

Somehow he couldn't turn into the pitch blackness of the second tunnel.

He kept on. The blue light led him past other side tunnels. Maybe one of them would lead him to safety, but he was committed now. He even tried to sing again.

Happy we are . . .

His voice was a faint creak of sound.

a-wandering . . .

His singing broke off. A sense of guilt swept over him. The blue glow leading him on reminded him of the blue of the marvelous shoe that his master Grel had made!

"I'm sorry!" he cried aloud. "I'm sorry I took that stone!"

The light floated farther along the tunnel, and he staggered after it. Tears blurred his eyes. "Forgive me!" he croaked.

The light floated on.

Just then, he thought he heard a distant *chunk, chunk, chunk*, like the sound of a pick biting into earth.

Chunk, chunk, chunk, chunk . . .

A muffle of voices.

Hap cried, *"Here! In here!"* He pounded on the wall of the tunnel.

Chunk, chunk, chunk . . .

A tiny opening appeared, sending a spear of light into the dark.

"Hurry!" Hap thought he was shouting, but his voice was like a vague wind in an empty house. Still, it was enough to spark excited arguing on the other side.

The hole widened. An eye appeared. An Auki eye. Sharp blue.

"Heolp ure freond," Hap croaked, sinking to his knees.

The digging resumed, faster than before. The words "Help our friend" had been heard. Finally, the hole was wide enough, and Hap struggled through, with Baen still over his shoulder.

He looked around, taking in a firelit cavern and a half dozen Aukis staring up at him. He was aware of hands lifting Baen and laying him gently on the ground. A female Auki knelt down, wiping the dirt from Baen's face. Her hand felt for his pulse.

She looked up.

"Hae ben dead."

"No!" Hap cried.

He swayed uncertainly. His knees buckled.

Twenty

HAP WOKE TO find himself gazing into the eyes of an Auki maiden with a delicate blue complexion, nicely pointed ears, and a thick growth of fluffy brown hair along her arms.

She turned, smiling, to the others. "Hae weccan!" ("He awakens!")

An elder came over and stared at Hap. His complexion was a darker, dirtier blue than the others'. But what struck Hap most was the length of the creature's nose. It was abnormal, even for Aukis, who were known for their impressive noses, and it curved up instead of down.

He pointed it now at Hap. "Ye speak ure *wort-hord?*"

Hap nodded. He did speak their "word hoard," as Aukis called their language—well enough, at least, to be understood.

These creatures, he learned, living in the deepest caverns, were the free Aukis. Some of them had never been enslaved by humans, while others, like the elder, had escaped from slavery and taken refuge here. He had even, Hap later learned, been away from the mountain once—just once—and had seen enough free-ranging humanity to last a lifetime.

Still, the boy was a surprise. He was mostly hairless, like the rest of mankind, and gigantically tall, but he didn't fit the Auki idea of human beings. To these creatures, he seemed almost "Auk-ward," meaning well brought up. And he had tried to save one of their kind! This was not human behavior. Still, they kept their children back, in case he should turn dangerous.

"Trinknst," the maiden urged, holding out a steaming bowl of soup.

Hap tried to sit up, but a sharp pain in his side took his breath away. He looked down and saw a bandage of sorts, made of dried mud. Evidently, he'd been unconscious for some time.

Carefully, he took the heavy earthen bowl, blew on the steam, and took a sip. He could tell the broth was strengthening, but it was also horribly sour and had some suspicious-looking stringy things in it, almost like the tails of rats. With a start, he realized that that was *exactly* what they were.

Politely, he set the bowl aside. "Do you have some plain water?"

The girl brought it, and Hap drank gratefully.

Slowly, the male Aukis approached. They crouched around him while the tribe's elder, whom they called Sheadu Raedr, asked questions. He seemed the only one among them who spoke human. He spoke it quite well, considering that he'd learned it in prison.

How many humans were there on the mountain? he wanted to know. What kind of weapons did they have? Where did they store them?

Hap answered honestly, although he knew very little about weapons caches. But he grew wary. Why, he asked, did they want to know these things?

"To kill humans" was the response.

Hap recoiled. Did he mean kill *all* humans?

Sheadu Raedr—his name meant "Shadow Reader"—seemed surprised at the question. Humans, he said, had enslaved the race of Aukis. They had imprisoned him—tortured him, in fact—and were busy ripping sacred gems from the holy mountain. Even now, they were in hot pursuit of the Great Blue, the holiest and brightest gem of all, hidden in the center of the earth. It was the duty of every Auki, he explained, to guard this treasure with his life and mislead the humans whenever possible. Why shouldn't they be killed?

"Then you should kill me," Hap said reasonably.

"Ye are a 'dyrne beorn,' as we say, a 'mysterious warrior.' We don't understand how ye came to be so inhuman."

"But I'm *very* human. Many of my kind are prisoners on this mountain, slaves like your own tribe. Most are not evil at all."

"I was in Slag's prison. I know what humans are."

"I cannot help you," said Hap firmly, "if you are going to kill my friends."

The old Auki stood and went to the fire. From a small ratskin purse, he extracted a handful of herbs and cast them into the flames. Immediately, the fire flared up, casting wild shadows on the cavern wall. Narrowing his eyes, the elder contemplated the twisting shapes. Much of his wisdom and authority, Hap would learn, came from his ability to read the meanings of shadows.

He stood a long while. It wasn't easy, apparently, to decipher the messages. Finally, he returned.

"The shadows tell what we know already," he said, "that the mountain is hurting." He gave Hap a stern look. "It is because of what the humans are doing."

"Yes," said Hap, "I feel it, too." He did. It was strange, but being inside the mountain, he could feel its life, almost its heartbeat. He felt it as an obscure sorrow, as if each blast of dynamite or stab with a pick opened another wound.

"The shadows also tell me to help ye. I do not understand this."

"Why? Because I am human?"

"Yes."

Hap decided to take a chance. "You have wisdom," he said. "You are able to read the shadows. But you are wrong about us."

"So ye have said."

"There are good people and bad. From what I've seen, it is true of Aukis as well."

The elder lowered his ruglike brows. "It is not for ye to judge us," he said. "Ye have not been oppressed. Nor spat upon."

"Actually," said Hap, "I have. And by Aukis."

"I am sorry for that."

"But I know there are good Aukis. You, for instance. And Baen Hus. Also the ferryboat captain who took me here."

"Who did ye say?"

"His name is Ulf, and he's—"

Abruptly, Shadow Reader stood up. The fur on his shoulders was stiff.

"What is it?" said Hap.

The creature looked into the darkness. "I cannot help you more."

"What did I do?"

"Ye spoke a forbidden name."

"All I said was that the ferry captain—"

"Speak it not twice!" Shadow Reader turned to face the boy. "Go. Our warriors will show the way."

Hap couldn't believe this. He'd been doing so well. "But the shadows told you to help me."

"I did not read them well."

"You read them perfectly," said Hap daringly. "What are you afraid of?"

"No fear," replied the Auki. "But the one ye speak of is dead to us."

"Dead?"

"He married a human!"

"If you ever met Mag, you wouldn't—"

Shadow's brows again lowered. "Ye *know* this woman?"

"She saved the life of my friend."

The elder looked into the fire as if for answers. "Many friends ye have."

"Not so many I can afford to lose one."

Shadow nodded. "True."

"Anyway," said Hap, "regardless of what—" He stopped himself before he spoke Ulf's name. "Regardless. We need to remember what is important."

"Is his offense not important? To choose a human?" He spat.

"Perhaps you're right," said Hap, trying to calm him. "But the person we should talk about is Slag."

The elder flinched at the name.

"Yes," said Hap. "He is the enemy. But we've been fighting separately. We cannot win this way."

Shadow Reader was trying to read the boy as he would the shapes on the wall. "This is true," he said at last.

"I will show you some humans who want to help in this fight."

"I do not speak to humans."

"Then speak through me," he said. "I know your language. Some of it."

Shadow pulled thoughtfully on the end of his nose. "I have hated the humans long and long time. I cannot think differently."

"Then we lose."

The old Auki was struggling between what he knew and what he was learning. "I need to consult the shadows."

Shadow Reader's confusion was painful to watch. "I know it is hard to stop hating," said Hap. "But you don't hate me, I think."

"No," he said. "Unfortunately."

"We have to trust each other."

"Trust?" The old one glanced around at his little group of followers, the males crouching expectantly, the women behind, and by the far wall the Auki children gazing with big eyes.

"I will obey the shadows," he said. "We will see if trust comes later."

In the hour that followed, Hap learned a great deal. The free Aukis, it turned out, wandered through the mining areas at times when no one was about. They had a collection of human artifacts that they'd picked up there, including a boot without laces, an old woolen shirt, and several sticks of dynamite.

Hap also learned about the tunnels. Many were unknown to humans, although they ran everywhere through the mountain. Those close to the surface were seldom used, the danger of capture being too great.

There was even a tunnel running beneath the building Slag used as a jail.

Hap looked up sharply.

"This interests ye?" said the elder.

"Very much." Hap explained Sophia's plight.

"This is your *luf-wif*?"

"My wife? I'm only a kid!"

"At your age, I was a grandfather."

Hap looked at him to see if he was joking. He wasn't. "I can see our lives are different."

"That is so."

"But still, you've *got* to help save her."

"Ye'd take such chances for one who is not your wife?"

"She's my friend."

"Ah." The old one nodded. "An *freond*. I have seen how ye treat friends: carry them for miles on your back through dark tunnels."

"If I have to."

"I am starting to trust you already."

Twenty-one

A LANTERN STOOD flickering on the bench, casting ghosts into the rafters and giving the prisoner's cheeks a glow they hadn't earned. The girl was, in fact, quite pale. Lack of food, lack of sunlight, and lack of happiness will do that.

Fear does it, too, and Sophia Hartpence was afraid, although she wouldn't want to admit it. Her nose was still red and sore from the vicious twisting they'd given it to make her talk, and her stomach was in knots from their efforts to starve her.

She decided to try one more time the magic spell for making feasts appear. It hadn't worked yet, but maybe she had it wrong. The problem was she was doing it from memory; she'd left the spell book somewhere and felt lost without it.

She raised her arms. "Murgudy, burgurry . . . ," she began. She was too hungry to think but stumbled on.

Just then, the clump of approaching boots grew louder in the hall. Then soldiers arrived and jangled open the cell. Behind them strode Slag himself. He stood for a moment, observing his captive. A smile quirked at the corner of his mouth.

"Hungry?" he said, taking off his hat and stepping in. "Silly question. After two days, who *wouldn't* be hungry?"

Sophia was, in fact, crawling with hunger.

At Slag's signal, a servant boy appeared with a small table and two folding chairs. He was followed by another servant, who snapped open a white linen cloth. The table was set for two, complete with candle and long-stemmed rose.

Then the food arrived. Ah, the food: a covered dish from which the aroma of roast lamb enticingly escaped, a platter of rainbow trout amandine, roasted potatoes, warm corn pudding, tiny cakes, glasses of hot cider with cinnamon sticks to stir with.

Sophia felt faint. Her hands groped along the wall for support. Was it possible her spell had worked?

"Join me, won't you?" Slag pulled out a chair.

Two days—forty-eight empty-bellied hours—with only a pitcher of stagnant water to sustain her. "What do I have to do?"

"Do? Why nothing at all, silly girl! Come!"

She staggered forward. *It's the magic,* she thought. *It's the magic!*

He shoehorned her into the chair.

Up close, the steam tickled her nose, and the smells hummed seductively.

"Before we begin . . . ," said Slag, taking the seat opposite and settling the hat back on his head.

Her fork, reaching for a slice of lamb, paused in midair.

"You must tell me how to address you. You know my name, but I don't know yours."

The juice was oozing. The potatoes were sizzling.

"I know you don't," she said, and again reached her fork to stab something wonderful.

"But . . ."

The fork again paused.

"But it's not polite. If we're having dinner together . . ."

"I like to be mysterious."

"Ah," said Slag, moving the platter just out of reach, "but, you see, I don't."

Her fork swung like a compass needle toward the broiled trout. Slag pulled that away, too.

"Your name."

"Cleopatra."

Slag nodded to the serving boy, who took away the fish dish. Sophia watched in dismay.

"For every false answer, we will subtract one dish."

The girl was silent, contemplating him. Under his hat, he was bald—she knew that—but the angles of his face still added up to handsome. Could someone who looked the way he did really be so cruel?

"Your name," he said again.

"Ludmilla."

Away went the lamb.

"Your name!"

Tears stood in the girl's eyes. Her whole body was aching. "You're a beast," she whispered.

"That's not a name."

"My name is Sophia!" she snapped. "So what?"

"Sophia what?"

"Sophia Hartpence."

"You may take a bite. Anything you wish." He spread out his arms.

She speared a crusty bit of roast potato and popped it in her mouth. She closed her eyes to savor its amazingness.

But instead of making her less hungry, it made her more. Much more.

"Uh-uh!" tutted Slag as she reached for seconds. "We have a few more questions first."

She looked as if she would stab him with the fork.

The candle flame doubled in Slag's eyes as he leaned forward. "Why did you come to the mountain?"

"I thought it looked picturesque. *Now* can I have more?"

The potatoes went away. Sophia watched tragically.

"Why did you come to the mountain? We know you were smuggled in. We want to know why."

Sophia was staring at a puffy chocolate tart.

"Sophia?"

She looked up. "I wanted to help a friend."

"Help him how?"

"That's two questions."

Slag smiled. "Quite right. You may have the tart."

She snatched it up before he could change his mind. But no sooner had she swallowed it than she felt hungrier than ever. She had never felt so hungry in her life!

"Help him how?"

"Help him escape! Now let me at that corn pudding!"

"One spoonful."

She scooped as much as her little spoon would hold but in her haste dribbled half of it on her chin. The part she swallowed made her ravenous for more.

"Say," she said, "what did you put in there?"

"Our chef has a special ingredient he uses for these occasions."

"It's making me hungrier with every bite!"

"Perceptive."

"Why are you doing this?"

"You've heard the saying 'a good appetite makes the best seasoning'? My cook believes the reverse: Good seasoning makes the best appetite."

"Not fair!"

"Perhaps not. So tell me, Sophia. You don't mind me calling you Sophia, do you? What was your friend's name again?"

"Who?" Her eyes were fixed on a glass of cider. A sudden thirst swept over her. Her throat felt as though it had been rubbed with sandpaper.

"Your friend. The one you want to save."

"Just a sip."

"Your friend."

"One little sip!"

"His name!"

"Hap Barlo!" The words flew out of her mouth before she could stop them.

She closed her eyes in despair. "Oh no," she murmured. "I didn't mean—"

"Barlo!" Slag shook his head. "Well."

"I didn't mean that! I meant . . . Fat Marlow."

"It doesn't matter."

"Fat Marlow's his name!"

"It doesn't *matter*, I tell you. He doesn't need saving anymore."

She frowned, confused.

"Hap Barlo died today in an explosion."

Her face froze.

"Now," he said, tenting his fingers, "just a few more questions and we'll enjoy our meal."

She stared at him blankly.

"Why were you climbing through my window the other night?"

Sophia's mouth opened, but no sound came out.

"Are you listening? I asked you why . . ."

He never found out. The prisoner's eyes closed, and she slid from the chair onto the floor.

Twenty-two

SLAG WAS IN a black mood when he returned to headquarters. He became even more irritable hearing the guffaws of soldiers in the back room. A bowl of ale was fine
once in a while, but didn't they have any Blueskins to
abuse or prisoners to punish?

You'd think they were here for their amusement!

Not even the sweet tenor voice of Silas Barlo, half
drowned out by shouts, could improve his mood. As
for that girl, she obviously knew more than she'd said. You
don't climb through windows at midnight for the exercise!

Maybe he'd used too much appetite-enhancement
powder. Who'd have thought she'd faint? The weakling!

He kicked his desk, splintering the veneer. That made
him even angrier.

Just then came a knock at the door. Two soldiers

174

entered with a furious woman held tightly between them. Her head was down like a charging bull.

"What's this?"

"A spy, sir," said one. "We caught her passing information."

"Spy, my eye!" growled the female.

Slag ducked his head to look at the face under the mop of hair. "You must be mistaken," he said to the soldier.

"I'm afraid not, sir."

"This is one of my best workers. She's been heading up the kitchen staff for years. I trust her completely."

The woman raised her head. It was Gert, the formidable being who doled out slop to miners each evening. "Thank you, Mr. Slag," she said. "I'm glad somebody is showing sense."

"That's all right, Gert," he said. "We'll get to the bottom of this." He gave the soldiers an impatient look.

The one who'd spoken before cleared his throat. He handed the chief a small wad of paper. "This fell out of her apron pocket. Good thing I noticed."

The paper was folded tight as a claw. Slag pried it open. His frown deepened as he read:

" 'S. knows where it is. Two days at most. Game starts Sunday 6:15 a.m.' "

He looked up. "But this is treason!" He rubbed his chin. "At least, I *think* it's treason."

The soldier nodded. "Does look like it."

Gert didn't seem to be paying attention. She was

listening to the voice in the other room singing of sunny summer mornings in old Aplanap.

"Game," Slag murmured. "At six in the morning? Who plays games at six in the morning?" He turned to Gert. "Where did you get this? Who were you giving it to?"

"Never seen it before. Somebody must've slipped it in my apron."

"Gert, that won't do."

"It's true!"

"What's this about a 'game'?"

She shrugged.

"Am I to understand that the S stands for my name?"

"I never thought about that."

"What's going to happen Sunday morning?"

She shook her head helplessly.

"I'm disappointed, Gert." He gave a brief nod to the soldiers. "Put her in one of the holding cells. We'll work this out later."

After they'd gone, Slag paced his office. The singing in the next room was grating on him. First a girl tries to break into headquarters, then a trusted staff member, whom he's known for years, is caught with a treasonous message.

If not treasonous, obscure. A code of some kind. Who uses codes but traitors?

He gave his desk another kick.

Chunk, chunk, chunk . . .

An insistent rhythm was intruding on Sophia's dream.

At first, she thought it was a drum. There was a parade of some sort. Not a very happy one. Slow as a funeral march.

Whose funeral? she wondered as she watched the mourners passing on foot, their faces covered in veils.

Chunk, chunk . . .

The drumbeat grew louder, closer. The parade was coming toward her. She frowned and opened her eyes, suddenly awake. Her heart fell when she realized where she was. She preferred the funeral.

But what was this? A small hole had appeared in the floor of her cell. As she watched, it grew larger, pieces of rock falling away into the darkness.

Somebody was down there!

She crawled over to see.

The noise stopped. Part of a face appeared in the opening. Even covered with dirt, it looked familiar.

"Is that you, Sophia?"

"Hap?" Relief swept through her. *"Hap!"*

"Hold on, we're coming. Stand back."

"It's you."

"Who did you think?"

What she'd thought, for only a second, was that he was dead and his ghost was climbing out of the grave.

"Stand back, Sophia, I mean it."

Chunk, chunk, ker-crack!

A foot-wide hunk of the floor suddenly fell out of sight. A second later, Hap's head popped up, disgracefully dirty and smiling like the devil. "Hey!" he said.

"Hey," she said back. She was not going to cry. That was definite.

Another few inches of flooring crumbled away. Hap's hands reached up and got a grip. A moment later, he was in the cell with Sophia.

"You okay?" he said. "Why are you crying?"

"I am *not* crying, Hap Barlo."

He studied her face. "You look a little wobbly. Did they hurt you?"

"Not badly. Mostly, they starved me. And they told me you got blown up!"

"I did," he said, pleased. "But then I fell into a tunnel, and I started following it, and there were all these rats, you couldn't see a thing, but you could hear them all around, and there was this blue light. . . ."

Sophia had very little idea what he was saying.

"Oh," said Hap, "you've got to meet my friend. Shadow, come on up."

Slowly, the Auki elder emerged from the darkness. Sophia backed away. She'd never seen an Auki close up, except for Ulf, who'd been in human clothes, a sailor outfit. The first thing she noticed was the long nose and odd vinegary smell. Then there were his clothes—rags, really, and not many of them at that; they barely covered what they had to. Tangled hair twirled over his shoulders and arms, spared his chest, and began again with his legs. He didn't even have shoes. His feet, which she just glanced at, ended in claws.

"What did you call him?"

"His name's Shadow Reader. He's helping us."

She nodded warily. "Hello."

The elder nodded back.

A distant clang made everyone turn. A door was being unbolted. Footsteps approached along the corridor.

"Get back down!" whispered Sophia.

Shadow slithered out of sight.

"You too," she said.

"You first."

"No time!"

Hap nodded and squirmed into the darkness. Sophia dragged over the wooden bench and sat on it, just as soldiers arrived.

"In you go!" One of them gave Gert an extremely impolite shove that sent her sprawling.

Sophia held her breath until the key clanked and footsteps retreated.

"Gert?"

The woman looked up. "I'm too old for this," she said, touching her forehead where she'd hit the floor.

Sophia ran to her.

The woman tried for a smile but ended with a wince. "I'm all right. What about you?"

"Hungry as a bear. In fact, I could *eat* one."

Gert struggled to sit up. "They didn't use that appetite-enhancement trick, did they?"

"Is that what they call it? They sure did."

"My dear, we've got to get some food in you!"

"I know. It's getting worse."

"It will. That stuff will eat away your stomach lining! Drink some water!"

"Don't have any."

"Call the guard, he'll get you some."

"Gert, wait! That's not important now. We've got to get out of here."

"Well," said the big woman, "you still got your spirit. They didn't enhance *that* out of you."

"I mean it!"

"In case you haven't noticed, we're in jail."

"Not for long."

"Oh? How do you propose—?"

"Down here," came a muffled voice from under the bench.

"What?"

Sophia pushed the bench aside to reveal Hap's dirt-caked head, grinning.

Gert clasped her heart.

"This way, ladies," Hap said.

Twenty-three

"Two days at most . . ."

Slag clamped his eyes shut to concentrate. Unfortunately, he was still pacing the room and ran straight into the desk.

He gave it a vicious kick. The carpenter would be busy tomorrow.

"S. knows where it is. Two days . . ."

Slag. Sophia. Silas . . .

Not Silas, surely. A fool with a lucky voice.

Sophia? Possible.

But what if it stands for Slag? What do I know? What will happen two days from now that I know about?

He stopped in the middle of the room.

Impossible. No one knows that.

No one knows that I know.

Well, Maurice does. He has to oversee the work crews. Also, of course, the surveyor.

Three people on the whole mountain, Slag mused, knew where the gem was located. Three people knew how to reach it—and that it would take two days!

Three people—and Gert! The soup slopper from the mess hall!

For years, the image of the great diamond had hovered in Slag's dreams like a dancing blue light, leading him on. When the winds had howled like wolves around the crags, Slag had hung on, driving deadbeat prisoners and devious Aukis to dig faster, dig deeper, to the heart of this horrible mountain.

Now, when Slag was on the verge of success, the mayor of Aplanap had to poke his nose into things. The mayor knew of the gem and had ordered it brought back for his beloved Ludmilla.

That wasn't going to happen. Slag had discovered it, he'd destroyed lives to get to it, and he would *have* it!

But first he'd have to talk to Gert. It was obvious now that she was working for a group of traitors, passing them information she'd learned at headquarters.

There'd be no gentle "appetite enhancements" for her. Slag would put her on the rack!

The door leading to the holding cells creaked open on iron hinges. By now, Slag was used to the clammy air laden with sour smells, but his nose still gave an involuntary twitch as he grabbed a wall torch and started down.

Only three cells lined the corridor. In the first, coughing uncontrollably, lay an old shirker pretending to be suffering from blue lung. A week in solitary would take care of that!

In the second, slurping his gruel, crouched a thief who'd stolen another miner's shoes when his own had worn through. *We'll see how he likes going barefoot,* Slag thought.

At the end stood the cell with the two treacherous females.

What was this? They hadn't been moved, had they? He held the torch higher. The girl was nowhere in sight. And Gert? Ah, there she was.

Or *part* of her . . .

The top half of the woman was in the jail cell, where she belonged; the bottom half was in a hole in the floor. She was stuck!

Slag put his whistle to his lips and blew a shrieking blast. A moment later, he had the woman by her elbows and was pulling hard.

"Umpf!" puffed Gert.

She kept trying to wedge her considerable self into the hole in the floor while Slag struggled to pluck her out.

"I've got you, old girl! You can't escape!"

It was beginning to look like a draw when Gert suddenly twisted her head and bit Slag hard on the wrist.

He said something to her then that, on consideration, we will leave out of our story. Ask your parents.

But as bad as what he said was, what he did was worse. He grabbed poor Gert under her chin and yanked mercilessly hard. It wasn't clear what would happen. Either he'd pull her back into the cell or her head would pop off.

At that moment, Slag was distracted by a flittering shadow overhead. Then something struck him hard. The cell spun dizzily as he fell.

Sophia stood over him. She was holding a shovel in her hand and watching a bump grow on his head. The thought crossed her mind that she should draw a face on the bump, so that her tormentor would have two bald heads, a big one and a little one. *Two heads*, she giggled, *are better than one.*

But there was no time for nonsense. She tossed the shovel aside and set to work pushing down on Gert's shoulders. From below, Hap and Shadow were pulling on her legs.

There was a soft *plock!* and Gert disappeared. A moment later, Sophia followed.

Slag lay sprawled on the stone floor, his mind somewhere between wakeful and woozy, until rough hands shook him and he opened his eyes. A guard was trying to rouse him.

"Oh!" Slag felt the back of his head. The shovel lay beside him. Smart as he was, he put two and two together and came up with a headache.

"Stop them," he groaned.

Soldiers ran to the jagged hole in the floor, and two managed to wriggle down into it before a muffled explosion suddenly knocked them flat, rattled the jail bars, and sent a great cloud of choking black smoke into the room.

PART FOUR

Silas

Twenty-four

HAP'S EARS WERE still ringing from the blast as he pulled Gert along with him through the tunnel. It would have been hard enough to see even without the smoke that left their eyes burning, but they were safe now. It would take days for Slag's men to dig through the dirt and rocks dislodged by the explosive charge.

Glancing ahead, Hap saw the silhouette of Sophia suddenly collapse.

"Sophia!" he called. Her strength had given out, and once again the boy found himself carrying a friend over his shoulder.

Twenty minutes later, dripping with dirt and smeared with soot, the little troop burst into the cavern of the Aukis to discover that a ceremony of some kind was in progress. At the sight of the intruders, the males let out ferocious yowls. They brandished picks and spears and even a few rocks that lay at hand.

Behind them, flickering candles encircled a platform where someone—someone quite short—lay wrapped in a blanket.

Hap looked questioningly at Shadow.

"Baen Hus," the old one explained.

The males, hearing the elder's voice, glanced at one another and began lowering their weapons. Several touched their foreheads and gazed briefly upward, the universal Auki gesture of respect. But they clearly didn't like the idea of humans in their midst.

"Steondan her," murmured Shadow, gesturing to Hap to back away.

"Baen was my friend, too," he answered.

Shadow merely shook his head. Humans were bad luck. They had no business in Auki rituals.

So Hap backed against the wall, where Gert helped him lower Sophia to the ground. The girl was awake but confused.

"We've got to get some food in her," said Gert.

Hap whispered to the elder, who nodded. One of the Auki warriors was called over, and soon a bowl of steaming rat-tail soup appeared.

"Here," said Hap, crouching beside Sophia and holding the bowl to her lips.

"What is it?"

"Wonderful stuff."

She took a sip, made a wry face, then sipped some more. She chewed unquestioningly on the gristly rat tails and soon had finished the whole bowl.

"Ah," she sighed, leaning back. "That was good. Got any more?"

But Shadow had already left to join the ceremony.

"Have to wait," Hap murmured.

She nodded. She seemed stronger than before and was sitting up. The three of them, half hidden by stalactites, watched in silence as the funeral resumed—the communal moan, the rolling about in the dust, the ritual slapping of faces, the shouted prayer to the goddess, and finally, the placing of gemstones on the eyelids of their fallen friend.

Six males then lifted the body and carried it to the Auki burial vault, after which each mourner stepped hard on his neighbor's foot for luck, concluding the ceremony.

Soon after, an Auki maiden appeared with another bowl of soup. Her eyes were red from crying and her cheeks pink from slapping. This time, Sophia was well enough to realize what she was eating.

"Oh, no thanks," she said with a slight shudder. "I couldn't drink another drop."

They made an odd-looking group: Hap, Sophia, Gert, Shadow, and two Auki warriors, sitting around a circular rock. At first, the warriors had trouble accepting the idea of working with humans. That is putting it politely. They spat on the ground. To get beyond a generation of hatred required all of Hap's skills. But in fact, he was his own best argument, for it was impossible not to like him. Had he not carried their beloved Baen Hus for miles through rat-infested tunnels?

The most conclusive argument, though, was time. There wasn't much of it. In two days, if their information was right, Slag and his gun-wielding goons would reach the Great Blue, the gem at the heart of the Auki religion. The slaves working in the mines did what they could to mislead their masters—digging in wrong directions, feigning illness, disabling machinery—but the traitorous Pec, the Auki foreman, always discovered what they were up to. Two days at most, and all would be lost.

The Aukis finally agreed to cooperate. What remained was to come up with a plan. Hap suggested they set up a meeting immediately.

"Let it be so," said Shadow.

Hap hesitated. "There is something you should know, Shadow. This meeting—"

"Hwaet?"

"I know there is someone whose name I should not speak."

The Auki's eyes narrowed.

"He may be there."

"Not!"

Hap sighed.

"No meeting with the traitor," Shadow flashed.

"Do you want Slag to win? Do you want to lose the Great Blue? It's your choice."

The elder and his warriors exchanged glances.

"Ye ask much."

The little group sat in silence.

At last, Shadow Reader lifted his head and nodded.

"You're not going without me," said Gert.

"Or me, obviously," Sophia put in.

Hap frowned. "You fainted last time, remember?"

"I was starving!"

"You're still too weak to travel."

Shadow shook his head. "Females," he muttered in Auki. "Bad luck in the tunnels."

The warriors nodded vigorously.

"What'd he say?" said Sophia.

"He said it sounds like a fine idea." Hap took the elder aside. In a low voice, he explained that it would save a lot of time to give in. "Look," he said, "you can't win an argument with Sophia. It can't be done. She'll wear you down, and you'll end up giving in anyway."

Aukis do not smile, but this one came close. "I think," he said, "she is your *luf-wif*."

"Please," said Hap, half laughing, "don't say that!"

"I see what I see."

"She's just my annoying friend. I'm telling you—"

"I think," said the Auki, "ye *want* her to come."

"That's crazy."

"So all right, she comes. And her large friend."

Hap gave up trying to convince the reader of shadows that he was not a reader of minds. His *luf-wif*!

Twenty-five

HAP HAD NEVER imagined what it would be like to hike up treacherous inclines in dark tunnels with two strong-minded women and three bossy Aukis, all talking at cross-purposes. Shadow and his warriors knew the mountain inside out and had the advantage of clawed feet. They scampered ahead, then had to wait while Hap slid about in his worn-out shoes and Sophia complained of stubbed toes.

The biggest challenge, Hap knew, was getting the word out about the meeting without alerting Slag's men. Now that Gert was a fugitive, she could no longer stroll into headquarters as she used to.

But her cousin Mag could—Mag, who was married to the much-hated ferry captain, Ulf.

Shadow wanted nothing to do with her. Wouldn't hear of it.

"You don't have to talk with her," countered Gert. "I'll get her the message, and she'll pass it to Silas."

"My father?" said Hap.

"Of course, your father. He's our contact."

Gert knew where Mag could generally be found—in the camp's laundry shed, where she worked when she wasn't driving the prison wagon. Reluctantly, Shadow showed the way that led there.

While he and the others waited below in the tunnel, Hap and Gert climbed a wobbly ladder to the shed. As Hap creaked open the trapdoor, the voices of women reached him through billowing clouds of steam.

But then he heard a male voice, the distinctive, strangely nasal speech of an Auki. That was odd. One seldom met with Aukis outside their tunnels. It was even rarer to hear them speak human.

This one sounded irritated. "Is it not Tuesday? Is not Tuesday the day for shirts?"

"Don't take that tone with me," answered a rough-voiced female.

Mag, Hap realized.

"The starch didn't come till this morning," she went on. "You know how your friend is about unstarched shirts."

"How long?"

"Ten, maybe fifteen minutes."

"Well, hurry. Mr. Maurice isn't used to waiting."

Maurice, thought Hap. *So this must be one of his errand boys.*

Now that he listened closely, he realized that he recognized the voice. It was that cruel little creature with the face like a rotted turnip, the one they called Pec. Hap still had a mark on his cheek from Pec's whip.

Gert was listening, too. She was just behind Hap on the ladder. This was a healthy-sized woman—"big-boned," as she liked to say. The ladder, if anything, was little-boned. A moment later, with a creak and then a crack, it gave way, and Gert thumped to the dirt below, nearly crushing Sophia. Hap managed to hang on by the upper rungs.

Above, silence.

Suddenly, the trapdoor flew open. Peering down was the fierce-faced Pec, his long nose wobbling. "You!"

Hap and Pec stared at each other, their minds racing in opposite directions. All Hap could think was that he had to stop this creature from calling the soldiers. He reached up and grabbed hold of a hairy ankle.

"*Craahhh!*" cried Pec, sounding like an angry crow. He pulled out his little whip and swung it down smartly, again and again, on Hap's hands and head.

Hap cried out but didn't let go. Instead, he pulled himself halfway into the room, hands bleeding but still holding on.

The whipping grew more frantic, and finally Hap's grip loosened. Pec hopped away as the boy struggled to his feet and stumbled after him out the door into the cold. It was no use. The Auki was speeding down the snowy path, hooting with glee.

The boy held his bloodied hand against his chest.

"Hap?"

He turned and saw Big Mag the mule driver. She was holding a white shirt in her hand.

"Here," she said, and wrapped the shirt, French cuffs and all, around his wound. She led him back in.

"What will Maurice say?" said Hap.

She shrugged. "He's got plenty of other shirts." She tore the cloth in strips and made a proper bandage. "Why'd you come? You're taking a chance."

"We need your help." Hap led her to the trapdoor and

called down to Gert.

The two women exchanged quick hellos, and Gert explained the plan.

Mag nodded. She was used to carrying messages. "And you're all right?" she said.

"Hip's a little sore. You should do something about that ladder."

"Complainer," said Mag pleasantly.

"Can you make it tonight?"

"With luck."

The women exchanged a look, and Hap was struck by how similar they were, with their heavy faces and short, curly hair. Neither could be called fat, but you wouldn't want to get on either's wrong side. Gert was known to crush walnuts in her elbow, and Mag (if the story could be believed) had once carried Jack the mule across a stream when the animal was spooked by the current.

"You take good care of my cousin, you hear?" said Mag, throwing Hap a pretend frown.

"I promise." Wincing, he managed to descend the ladder one-handed to the place where it had broken off and jumped the rest of the way.

Immediately, Sophia wanted to know what the bandage was about.

"Tell you on the way. Slag's men will be here any minute."

And so they were. In fact, Hap and the others almost didn't make it to their meeting that night. There was a close call with guard dogs and a partial tunnel collapse.

They had to double back several times to confuse their pursuers. The worst part was toward the end, when they'd safely reached the tunnel opening and realized the sun hadn't set. They were too close to Slag's headquarters to venture out in daylight.

"Did you say Mag will be seeing my father?" said Hap, huddling against the tunnel wall.

"She'll pass him a note," said Gert. "That's how they nabbed me. I was bringing him news to get out to the others."

"But isn't he a prisoner? How would he—?"

"He puts it in his songs. You didn't know that? He puts the news in code, so Slag won't figure it out, and then he sings it."

"And someone is listening?"

"We have people in the kitchen."

Hap shook his head in admiration.

"There's another way, too, but it's not always possible."

"What do you mean?"

"Heat pipes. Don't worry," she said, seeing his confusion. "One way or another, you'll have your meeting."

Hap hesitated. "Will he be there?"

"Your dad? They keep a pretty close eye on him. I don't know."

Hap took that to be a no. Another no. It gave him a grinding feeling in his stomach to think his father was so close but out of reach.

At last, it was dark. The little troop made their way up a moonless path to the ledge above Slag's headquarters.

There to meet them was Markie, his one good eye bright with welcome. "Hap! Well done!" he said, giving his friend a shove. "And this must be Sophia. Just as pretty as you said."

Hap objected, his face reddening. "I never—"

"So why are you blushing? Hi, Gert." They shook hands warmly.

At the sight of Shadow Reader, he touched his forehead and tilted his gaze upward, in the traditional Auki sign of respect.

The elder nodded cautiously.

"Sorry, that's all the Auki I know. It's gotten me through a lot of scrapes." He led the group to the cleft in the rock wall. As they went in, Sophia gave Hap a mischievous jab in the ribs.

"What's that for?"

She grinned. "You were blushing."

"Was not."

"Happy likes Sophie."

"Stop that."

Inside, Markie found a lantern in the usual place. He lit it and led the way, sending ghastly shapes against the walls. The way was familiar to Hap from the last time, but the farther he went, the more nervous he became. Nervous about Shadow, mostly. He'd warned him who would be at the meeting, but the old Auki was unpredictable.

As the path sloped downward, stalactites grew more numerous, suspended from the ceiling like an army of hanged men. A faint glow appeared ahead. A final twist in the path and then, sudden as a magic trick, the great cavern opened before them—the jagged ceiling, the bright fire in the central area, and . . . no one!

There was no one there! Shadow and his followers glanced around nervously, aware they were totally exposed. Slowly, they drew their knives.

If there was little trust before, there was less now.

"Markie," Hap whispered, "where is everybody?"

His friend held up his hand. For the next minute, the only sound was the crackling of cedar logs and the occasional creak of bat wings overhead. At last, a man's face appeared over a low stalagmite. Another head appeared, this one topped with a miner's cap. Then another face, and another. Before long, a dozen men and several women stood silently around the edge of the cavern.

Shadow Reader and his Auki warriors were in a crouch. Firelight glinted off their knife blades.

Hap turned to the Auki elder. *"Freondas,"* he said. "These are your friends."

Shadow did not look convinced. Before Hap had stumbled into his life, he'd had only the worst kinds of run-ins with humans.

The humans were equally doubtful. They didn't trust Blueskins. Ulf was the exception. They tolerated him because of Mag.

"Listen, everyone," Markie called to the miners, "we've got some nervous Aukis here. Let's just have our leader step forward. Mag, you come, too."

A large woman and a small, long-nosed, human-like creature stepped into the open. Ulf and Mag certainly made an odd couple, but the sight of them made Hap smile. The more he knew them, the more he felt they belonged together.

Obviously, Shadow didn't feel the same.

Hap kept glancing from one to the other. The contrast between Ulf's seaman's outfit and Shadow Reader's rags and skins was striking.

"I heard ye might be here," Shadow said, lowering his brow.

"I'm with the untergrund," Ulf replied.

"Ye mean, you're with the humans. Ye even smell human."

"I won't say what you smell like."

"Tell me, was there no Auki maiden that pleased ye? Did ye have to turn your back on your kind and marry—*this?*" The look he shot Mag was not printable.

Ulf's eyes narrowed. "Do ye insult my wife?"

"I question your taste."

"Still haven't changed, I see." Ulf's voice was steady, but muscles in his jaw were working.

"At least," said Shadow, "I know what side I belong on."

"What side is that?"

"There are only two: Auki and human."

"No, Shadow, that's where ye make your mistake. For you, everything is race."

"Everything *is* race. Aukis serve the goddess. Humans serve their greed."

"Wait. Listen to yourselves," Hap broke in. "We've got to work together."

"Work with *him?*" said Shadow.

Ulf spat. "He calls himself a brother!"

"Yes." Hap ducked in. "We're *all* brothers here, brothers and sisters working together."

"No," said Ulf. "I mean he's my *brother.*"

Hap looked from one to the other. Was it possible? The noses were indeed similar—long and upward-curling. Most Auki noses bent down. "Well," he said weakly, "all the more reason to get along."

"We *never* got along," said Ulf. "Even as an Aukling, he had to be the leader. Now he reads shadows and tells everybody how to live."

"Ye should listen!" Shadow snapped. "Look at yourself! Ye look ridiculous in those clothes."

"Please tell my brother," said Ulf, "that this meeting is over."

"No, wait!" Hap cried. "Remember why we're here!"

"It was a poor idea." He turned and started away, with Mag beside him.

"Let him go," said Shadow Reader. "We will fight without him."

"You'll lose!"

"Then we will die honorably, as Auki warriors." Shadow signaled to his followers, and they started up the path.

Hap could hardly believe what was happening.

Markie put a hand on the boy's shoulder. "You tried."

"What good is trying? Slag wins."

Shadow was now climbing past the stalactites, which looked more than ever like hanged men. At the other side of the cavern, Ulf's group was filing out through a back tunnel.

Suddenly, as if from everywhere at once, a voice rang out: *"Everyone! Stop!"*

Shadow paused a moment but then continued on. Ulf's men went on their way as well. Clearly, the voice wasn't coming from either group. It certainly wasn't coming from Hap.

"Stop!"

Again, nobody stopped.

"Before it's too late!"

Apparently, it *was* too late.

That's when the voice, giving up on words, rose to a high, sustained, and, it must be said, quite beautiful tenor note echoing through the cavern.

Everyone turned.

"Dad," Hap whispered. He looked around wildly, but the cavern was an echo chamber, the sound bouncing from wall to ceiling to floor and back again.

Then it was replaced by a different sound:

Whappity-whappity-whappity.

Whappity-whap!

It was his father's little drum, the one he'd played when he sang for the children of Aplanap long ago.

Shadow and his followers started back down, their eyes darting everywhere. Ulf and the miners paused. Some were turning around.

Whappity-whappity!

Whap-whap!

After long seconds, a figure rose from behind an outcropping of limestone, on the side opposite from where everyone had been looking. He was a slightly built man, with a crooked little nose and button-bright eyes—eyes that were fixed, just now, on Hap Barlo.

"Dad!" Hap cried out. Tears sprang to his eyes as he ran madly across the cavern and into his father's arms.

"Son," murmured Silas, clasping him tightly. "Son."

For seconds, neither could speak. Hap felt several

warm droplets land on his head. Then he heard his father strenuously clearing his throat.

"Listen, everyone!" Silas shouted. "Slag knows about your meeting! He's on his way here with his men! You've got to get out!"

"Then we fight him here!" Shadow answered sturdily.

"Not here. Not yet," Ulf said. "We're not ready."

His brother hesitated. He knew the need for strategy. He hadn't lasted this long in the mountain without it. "How," he said, "do we stop him?"

"One way," said Hap, who had been listening, "is to stop fighting each other."

The Aukis looked at him. A flicker of anger crossed Ulf's face, but it passed. "The human is right," he said.

A distant rumbling and a mutter of voices made everyone turn.

"They're here!" cried Silas. "Quick! Out the back tunnel!"

"I suppose," said Shadow, starting to run, "we can hate each other later, when this is over."

"And will," said Ulf. "But now hurry!"

Twenty-six

WITH ULF AND Shadow in the lead, the band of resistance fighters raced through the low tunnels. Where the tunnels split off into two and then four directions, the Auki leaders signaled to each other to divide up and head different ways, confusing their pursuers.

Sophia and Hap stayed with Silas, who was doing the best he could at the back of the pack.

"Come on, Dad, faster!"

Silas looked at his son and nodded, too out of breath to speak. Somewhere back in the tunnels, dogs were barking.

Ulf's group was almost out of sight by now, and the torch Markie carried was a distant flicker. If it hadn't been for a bluish glow in the tunnel walls, Hap would have had trouble seeing anything. As it was, the going was dim, and his father stumbled more than once.

"Come on, Mr. Barlo," said Sophia, helping Silas to his feet. "You can do it."

"Thank you, dear."

The barking was louder now.

They ran on. But Silas was slowing.

"Dad," said Hap, "climb on my back. It'll be faster."

Still gasping for breath, Silas shook his head. "Won't work. Leave me here. *Hurry!*"

"I'm *not* leaving you, Dad. I've just found you!"

"You have to, or we're all lost."

Hap didn't want to believe his father was right.

"Think of Sophia," said Silas, who was simply walking now, and not walking fast. "Take her and run. I'll be all right."

"No, Dad—"

"If you're worried about the dogs, don't. They know me."

"I can't leave you."

"You've got to! Tell me, though, quick. The revolt begins when?"

"The revolt?"

"In case I can't be in touch."

"Sunday morning, six-fifteen. But, Dad—"

The barking was dangerously close. There was no time.

"Six-fifteen. Good. Now go on!"

"No, Dad."

Silas looked at his son. "The dogs know me," he said. "But they don't know your friend. They'll rip her apart."

Hap stared. He didn't know what to do.

"Go, son."

"I'll come back for you, Dad. I promise!" Hap looked at his father through tear-bleared eyes, then hugged him hard, grabbed Sophia's hand, and ran.

The night passed miserably, as did most of the next day. Hap felt sick with guilt. Staying wouldn't have helped; he knew that—Slag would have had three prisoners instead of one. But he couldn't stop thinking about those dogs. Was his dad telling the truth when he said they wouldn't harm him?

Probably it was good that Hap and Sophia were kept busy. They worked with Ulf, Shadow, and the others, chipping holes at strategic points in the walls—walls that ran parallel to the tunnels being worked by the miners. The idea was to establish spy posts and monitor the excavations.

Working as quietly as they could, Sophia and Hap managed to create an opening a foot wide overlooking one of the deepest workstations in the mountain. Situated high in the tunnel wall, it gave them a downward view of the shackled miners. Since this was an Auki station, it was Shadow who squeezed through and dropped down among them.

When the foreman looked his way, Shadow bent to the work, chipping away at a slab of bluish rock. When the foreman strolled to the far end, Shadow whispered to the Aukis around him, instructing them to be ready and telling them what to expect.

With metal clippers, he cut through their shackles. Cut through but didn't cut off. To the foreman, it would seem that the workers were still hobbled by chains.

While Shadow was busy in this station, Ulf was doing the same in another. He'd changed out of his captain's outfit, thrown on some rags, and become to all appearances just another Auki slave.

Markie, meanwhile, had slipped into a human workplace. The men there weren't in chains, because there was no danger of their escaping into the mountain. To Aukis, the mountain was home. To men, it was prison.

The problem was timing. The revolt, to be successful, would have to start everywhere at once. The plan they worked out was a long shot, but the only chance they had.

The next morning, quite early, Hap and Sophia stationed themselves beside a spy hole and watched. No one noticed them. The workers were all concentrating on a pulsing blue glow emanating from the wall.

"Careful!" cried a nasal voice that Hap recognized at once. It was Pec, and he had out his little whip, which he was wielding on the hairy backs of his fellow Aukis. "Clumsy vermin! I told you not to use picks! We don't want to break through yet."

A commotion behind him made Pec turn. He was

greeted by a strange sight: a couch carried on poles by four young Aukis. Sitting upon it, with a glass of iced tea in his hand, was Maurice the overseer, the same personage who had welcomed Hap on his first day in the mine.

"Morning, all," he said cheerily as the workers set him down. "I understand we are getting close. Is this the place?"

Pec ducked his head quickly several times in imitation of a bow. "It is. Yes, sir."

"Awfully hot in here. The ice in my tea is all melted away. You know how I hate warm tea."

"I do, Maurice. We'll remedy that when we get back."

"We'll just have to endure. As you may know, Mr. Pec, we're having a visitor. He's on his way as we speak."

From their hiding place, Hap and Sophia glanced at each other. "Get the others," whispered Hap. "Ulf, if you can find him."

Sophia set off at a run.

Hap checked the time. It was ten past six, Sunday morning. If something was going to happen, it would happen soon. He went back to watching, his heart thumping. As if in sympathy, the strange light continued its slow pulsing, dimmer and brighter, dimmer and brighter.

Just out of his line of sight, he heard a muffle of voices, and then a man strode in, accompanied by armed soldiers. Hap, from his odd angle, couldn't see his face, only the familiar bent-brim hat.

Slag's hat.

The Aukis backed off, their shackles jingling, as the big man made his way to the wall.

For some seconds, he said nothing, just taking it in. Then he turned, and Hap saw that it was indeed Slag. "Remarkable," he said. "You can almost see through the wall."

"True," said Maurice with satisfaction. "It is thin here. We wanted to wait for you before we broke through."

"Well done. Are we ready, then?"

Hap had to hold himself back from shouting, "Stop!" The time he'd spent inside the mountain had given him a strange feeling for the place. It seemed alive, and Slag's relentless pursuit of the Great Blue felt like a deadly assault.

Still no Ulf or Sophia, or help of any kind. Hap could do nothing but watch as Slag pushed an Auki roughly aside, took up a pick, and swung it full force against the translucent wall.

It shattered like heavy glass.

Hap's breath caught in his throat. It was as if he'd been struck himself.

With the wall gone, a sudden blinding geyser of blue light flooded the work site, along with a wave of heat. Everyone fell silent. Several Aukis knelt. Slag himself stood wide-eyed, one hand over his heart, as if instinctively protecting his vital organs.

Before them, cradled in surrounding rock, glimmered an immense blue diamond.

Slag spoke a single word: "Mine."

"Well, of course," said Maurice, blinking nervously, "we're in a mine. We're mining. And we know that we're mining for our mayor back in Aplanap." He gave Slag a significant look.

Slag didn't reply. He took off his hat. Was it in homage, Hap wondered, or because it was so hot down there? Slag's bald head looked blue in the strange light. Sweat glistened on its dome.

"Five years. Five wretched years on this mountain." He shook his head. "Beautiful, isn't it?"

"Oh, quite," said Maurice, "but how shall we transport it? Back to *Aplanap*." Again, a significant look.

Slag ignored him. "Is it true," he murmured, "what they say?"

"What? Immortality? Omniscience? Omnipotence?" Maurice chuckled. "I hardly think—"

"Let's find out," said Slag, wincing into the radiating light. "Maurice, why don't you step over and fetch it for me?"

The overseer's eyes bulged. "Oh, I couldn't. You should have the honor."

"I give the honor to you."

"Really, Mr. Slag, I—"

"Pick it up, Maurice. *Now!*"

Pec was hopping about excitedly. "Yes, yes, pick it up, pick it up, Maurice!"

"Mr. Pec," Maurice muttered, "I would thank you to keep your thoughts to yourself."

Just then, Sophia returned, out of breath. Ulf and

Shadow were with her, with others close behind. "What's going on?"

Hap nodded toward Maurice.

Ulf looked horrified.

"They mustn't!" Shadow hissed.

Hap shook his head. The hole he and Sophia had made in the wall was narrow. And what if they did manage to squeeze through? Slag's guns waited below.

"If you please," said Slag, nodding to the overseer.

Maurice's blinking was out of control, and he seemed to have trouble breathing. He extended a trembling hand, then drew it back.

"That's the idea," said Slag.

The overseer bit his lip. With sudden resolve, he reached out with both hands for the jewel.

There was a loud *snap!* followed by a burning smell, and Maurice was flung backward and lay in the dirt.

Pec ran around him in frantic circles. "Mr. Maurice, Mr. Maurice!"

"Then it's true," Slag murmured. "The gem *is* protected." He called one of the soldiers, who brought over a leather bag. From it, Slag took a pair of oversized gloves. They seemed oddly heavy, and he had trouble getting them on.

"Let's see if lead-lined gloves will help."

He reached out slowly, then hesitated.

Taking a deep breath, he relaxed his shoulders and was about to reach out again when a strange sound caught his ear.

It was a voice, a man's voice—singing.

Happy we are a-wandering,
it's what we care for most. . . .

Maurice, coming back to consciousness, began to groan. Clearly, he wasn't the singer. No, the voice, echoey and eerily beautiful, was coming—was it possible?— through the heat pipes.

For just because we're wandering,
it does not mean . . .

The end of the verse was lost, because all of a sudden, the air was rent with shouts and a loud clashing of chains as the Aukis flung off their shackles. One of them, growling fiercely, leaped on Slag's back, punching and biting. Others, shouting Auki oaths, pounced on the soldiers. A gun went off, but the man who fired it was immediately covered in Aukis. He fell, still struggling to shake free of them, and was lost in a snarl of fur.

Another soldier began backing away, firing shots as he went. An Auki fell to the dirt, clutching his shoulder.

"*Nan!*" cried Shadow. "*No!*" And he pushed Hap roughly aside. Wedging himself through the narrow hole, he dropped to the ground. Ulf quickly followed.

"It's happening!" yelled Sophia, giving Hap a triumphant hug.

"Yes," he said. "Now, run to the next spy hole and see if they heard the same thing. Markie, you go the other way. Quick!"

Without a word, the two of them sprinted off, checking every spy hole down the line. Each workplace had a pipe that drew heated air to the buildings above. And through each of these pipes, Silas's resonant voice had triggered violence. Shouts and shots, crashes and cries, reverberated through the tunnels.

The revolt was under way.

Twenty-seven

SLAG'S EYES WERE a flash of steel surprise as he ripped the Auki from his shoulder and flung him against the wall. Quickly, he reached out and closed his gloved hands over the great diamond, rocking it back and forth till it broke free. He slid it into the leather bag.

Shadow growled deep in his throat and started toward him.

"Be careful!" Ulf shouted, but his brother wasn't listening. His eyes were fixed on the bag.

Hap slithered through the opening in the tunnel wall. "He's got a gun!" he shouted, dropping to the ground.

So he had, and in a moment, it was out—a short, broad-snouted shotgun—pointed at Shadow Reader's heart.

"Well, well," sneered Slag, "the Blueskin wants to protect his precious jewel."

"Shadow! Get down!" yelled Hap, but the Auki kept going.

"*Steop, Sheadu!*" called Ulf.

"It's *mine!*" Slag shouted. "And I'll show you what I do to anyone who tries to stop me!"

Ulf and Hap were running and hardly noticed that Maurice was lying in their way. As Hap raced by, the overseer grabbed his ankle, sending the boy sprawling just as a gun blast rent the air.

Hap squirmed free and gave Maurice a kick in the gut, hard as he could, and heard a satisfying "*Oof!*" in response. Then Hap was running again, but in that brief time, the scene had changed. Slag had disappeared, along with Pec and two soldiers who'd managed to get away. Many of the Aukis were gone as well, giving chase. Those who remained were either wounded or tending the wounded.

That was when Hap saw Ulf and Shadow. His heart froze. The brothers were lying on the ground, and blood was sinking into the dirt beside them.

"No!" he cried, kneeling. The fur on both was sticky. "Talk to me!"

Ulf winced up at him, then closed his eyes. "Go after him," he said, his voice halting. "He's got the stone."

Shadow struggled to his hands and knees. "*Ulf!*"

In a soft gabble of Auki, Ulf tried to assure his brother

that he was all right, although it was obvious he wasn't. Listening to them, Hap understood what had happened. At the last instant, Ulf had thrown himself against his brother, knocking him to the wall just as Slag's gun went off. It was Ulf, not Shadow, who'd been hit.

"Where are you hurt?" said Hap.

"Is nic important."

Shadow turned sad eyes from Ulf to the human boy. "Go. I'll take care of my brother."

They were right, but knowing that didn't make Hap feel less guilty. For the second time in as many days, he was abandoning ones he cared about.

"Come on, Hap," said a voice behind him. "We better go."

It was Sophia, pink-cheeked and out of breath.

He didn't bother to argue.

Mount Xexnax was harder to get out of than into, especially if you were in a hurry. Slag and his guards jumped on the rattling, hand-operated elevator platform that would take them to the next level, where mules waited to carry them to the funicular railcars. When the system had been designed, decades earlier, speed had not been a consideration. Now, with newly freed Aukis and humans in furious pursuit, it was.

"Hurry!" Slag shouted as his men yanked on the chains that lifted the platform. He grabbed a section of chain himself and heaved into the work. They were just above the miners' reach now and rising. Fists were raised and shovels flung, but no use.

"You want us?" Slag yelled down. "Too bad. Tell you what. I'll give you one of your own."

With that, he grabbed Pec by one leg and held him over the side of the lift.

"Oh no, sir, you wouldn't hurt poor Pec," cried the Auki, his yellow eyes bulging. "Not Pec, not good, honest Pec."

"Goodbye, good, honest Pec."

Slag dropped him into the angry mob below.

There was a cry and a scuffle of fur, and nothing was seen of Pec again.

Jumping out at the next level, Slag lashed the elevator in place so that it wouldn't descend. "Come on!" he shouted, heading up the tunnel to where the mules were penned.

Below, several Aukis had begun climbing the elevator shaft, their clawed feet digging into the surrounding rock to steady them.

"Hap!" said Sophia. "Didn't we dig a spy hole around here?"

"You're right!" Hap called to the others: "There's a tunnel next to this one. Follow us!"

Hap and Sophia squeezed through a narrow opening, then scrambled up the tunnel's incline, followed by a dozen miners, both Auki and human. No torches were there to guide them, only the dull blue glow of the rock itself; but it was enough. No one spoke, Hap noticed. The friction between the races seemed to have been forgotten in their haste.

The little ragtag army emerged at last near the surface, where the tunnel joined the entryway to Portal Three. A blast of cold air greeted them as they stared out at Slag and his men climbing from the railcar and starting on foot up the snow-crusted path to the building marked "XCC."

This was not good. There would be soldiers in Command Central, lots of them maybe, and an arsenal of weapons.

"Wait!" cried Sophia, raising her hands high over her head, then lowering them halfway, like wings, and rotating them in tight circles.

The miners stared at her.

"By the power of Xexnax!" she shouted, and proceeded to utter a garbled collection of Auki-like consonants and throat clearings.

"*Not now*, Sophia!" said Hap. "This is no—"

But then his voice died out.

Slag had slipped and fallen. His two soldiers were also having trouble keeping their footing. One of them actually began sliding face-first down the hill. Before he could get to his feet, the Aukis caught him and pinned him.

"What did you *do?*" said Hap.

Sophia looked confused. "I don't know. I thought I was doing the 'Bees-in-Underpants Spell.' "

"Well, I wish you'd—whoa!" Hap cried as he slipped and fell hard on the ice.

"Actually," said Gert, who had just caught up with them, "it rained last night."

"You mean . . . ?" said Sophia.

"You know how slippery it gets when rain freezes."

"Come on," said Hap, seeing Sophia's disappointment. "We don't need spells to catch them."

The footing may have been tricky for humans, but the claw-footed Aukis scrambled ahead and began closing the gap with Slag.

Suddenly, a gunshot echoed across the frozen crust. Slag was facing them with his shotgun. "Stand back, or I'll blast your heads off!"

The miners stopped.

"Stay there and stay alive!" Slag yelled.

He hitched the leather pouch higher on his shoulder and began climbing again, the remaining soldier just behind him.

"We can't let them get to headquarters," said Gert, breathing hard.

"What do we do?"

She shook her head. Guns were guns.

"We keep going," said Markie firmly. "Keep down. And keep trees between you when you can."

That's what they did. Slag's soldier turned and fired off occasional shots, but he and his master were intent on making it to the building. And they were getting there. A minute later, Slag had his foot on the bottom step, his hand on the newel post. His grin seemed to say, "No one can catch me now!"

"Welcome," came a calm voice from above.

Slag stared into the shadowed porch. "Who's up there?"

A slightly built man stepped into a slant of sunlight.

"You!" said Slag.

"At your service." It was Silas Barlo, as pleasant as you please. "Any tune you'd like to hear?"

"What are you so cheerful about?" Slag thundered up the stairs. "Don't you know I can blow your head off?"

"Whatever you say."

"How'd you get free, anyway?"

"Everybody left. They seemed in a hurry."

"What do you mean, *they left?*" Slag brushed past Barlo and grabbed the door handle.

It didn't turn.

"Did you lock it?" he demanded.

"Yes, sir. I thought it would be a good idea. Keep out undesirables."

"Well, I'll take the key."

"I'm afraid I dropped it in the snow."

"Barlo, you're dead!"

Hap had now arrived, with the Aukis and others, at the foot of the stairs. They stared at the scene above them.

Slag yanked at the door. He pounded on it. "Why aren't they *answering?*"

"I told you." Silas smiled, and his crooked little nose wrinkled with amusement. "They heard there was trouble in the mine, so they went to help you."

"Went to help me? I never saw them there."

"That's odd. I told them where you'd be. Portal Two, right?"

"Portal Two? You idiot! We were in Portal Three!"

Slag turned and looked down from the porch. Dozens of humans and Aukis returned his stare.

Hap stepped forward. "Give up, Mr. Slag."

"Give up? *Give up?*"

"Really, sir. You might be able to shoot one or another of us, but these Aukis will tear you apart, I can assure you of that."

Slag turned to his remaining soldier, who was, to speak frankly, beginning to look a little pale. He didn't like the idea of being torn apart.

"Shoot him!" said Slag, pointing at Hap.

The soldier hesitated. "Who?"

"Shoot the boy!"

Sophia stood beside Hap. "You do and I'll tear you apart myself!"

"*Did you hear me?*" Slag roared. "Shoot him! Shoot them *both*!"

"I'd rather not, sir."

The commander stared. No one disobeyed him. Ever. He raised his shotgun and pointed it at Hap's head. "I'll do it myself!"

Then he changed his mind. Slowly, he turned and pointed the gun at Silas Barlo.

"All right," he announced. "Here is what's going to happen. You are all going to go away now. Otherwise, you will never hear this traitorous fellow sing another traitorous song."

Hap felt Sophia's hand tighten in his.

For several long seconds, there was silence on the mountain. Silas Barlo was loved. He was loved for his songs and for his courage in the resistance.

People even loved him for his funny little nose.

"Go ahead," said Silas calmly.

Slag frowned. "You're awfully brave."

"Not at all. It makes sense. You shoot me, the Aukis tear you apart, and the Great Blue is returned to the mountain where it belongs. It all works out rather well."

"You're an interesting fellow."

"Thank you."

"But I have a different idea."

As the miners stared, Slag set down the shotgun, pulled on his lead-lined gloves, and reached into the leather sack for the diamond. He held it high over his head, as if to compare it in brilliance with the early-morning sun slanting over the snow.

"What do I need with guns and hostages? I have this!"

He laughed a terrible laugh.

"Look at you all!" he shouted. "You dare pursue me?"

Another laugh broke free from some deeply unfunny place inside him.

"Slaves and Blueskins! *Behold!*"

No one moved. It's possible no one breathed. Slag himself appeared hypnotized as he stared upward into the shifting lights in the heart of the jewel.

"You can't touch me; don't you realize that?"

Soon his eyes widened in astonished pleasure, and a slow smile lit his face.

"Yes," he hissed. "Yes, I understand!"

Suddenly, he whirled around, holding the gem at arm's length as if it were a dancing partner. "Ha-ha!" he crowed. "I understand! I understand everything!"

The Aukis backed away. Even his soldier stepped back.

"Nothing can touch me!" Slag's voice rang out. "Not ice or guns or fire. Not armies! Not those miserable Aukis who imagine they own this place."

"Should we rush him?" whispered Sophia.

Hap's mouth was open. "I don't know."

"And *certainly*," continued the wild man, "not that ridiculous mayor and his twice-ridiculous wife! To think they wanted my diamond!"

His eyes grew manic. "Now I rule the mountain! *All* the mountains!"

He held the jewel high and laughed. It began to glow more brightly than before. The lights within it were dancing.

But his laugh seemed to catch in his throat. Something was wrong.

"Ah—" he gasped.

Slag's head, blue with reflected light, grew oddly distorted. Bumps appeared on his bald skull, then on his forehead and cheeks.

"*Arrrrr!*" he cried, sinking to his knees.

The bumps grew larger, and then, as Hap watched,

229

transfixed, one of them burst, and sticky green liquid oozed down the side of his head.

Another burst, and another.

Slag screamed.

In minutes, what remained of the fearsome man was a slippery mess slowly darkening into ice.

The diamond, hot as blue flame, burned its way back into the mountain and disappeared.

PART FIVE

Xexnax

Twenty-eight

BACK HOME IN Aplanap, no one had a clue about any of this. In fact, with the newspaper shut down and tourists scarce, there wasn't any news at all. The truth is, people were discouraged. You'd be discouraged, too, with the clouds hanging heavy as mattresses and nothing to buy in the shops. Indeed, the town had become so quiet you could hear the faint tick and scratch of leaves as they landed on the glassy streets and slid downhill. Sometimes a twirl of wind lifted them in a spinning dance, then set them down in rustling piles against the sides of buildings.

But the day came finally when another sound was heard: the sharp *tock, tock, tock* of a walking stick. The townspeople looked out their windows as a dark figure trudged through the glass-coated center of town.

It was clearly a stranger. No one in Aplanap went about wrapped in a black hooded cowl that covered him from head to foot. And no one was that tall.

Curiosity got the better of people. Doors opened and the townsfolk ventured out—carefully, to be sure, holding on to postboxes and lampposts to keep from slipping.

On he continued, past the jeweler's shop, the cheese emporium, the baker's and clockmaker's, while behind him more people followed.

Near the top of the hill, beside the cliff overlooking Doubtful Bay, stood the cobbler's shop. The stranger paused. Everyone behind him stopped as well.

Lifting his stick, he rapped sharply on the door. "Come out!"

There was no answer. There was, in fact, no one there.

A boy was sent to bring Grel the cobbler, who was staying above the watchmaker's shop until he could find a place to live. Another messenger was sent sliding down to the Town Hall to alert the mayor.

Grel came quickly, tucking in his shirttails. His dog, Rauf, was with him, wiggling with excitement. It didn't take much to make Rauf wiggle.

"Ye are the cobbler," declared the stranger.

Grel nodded.

Beneath the shadow of the cowl, the man's eyes glittered. "Where," he said, "is my shoe?"

Grel was afraid. This was the day he'd hoped would never come. "It's inside."

"Get it!"

The cobbler retrieved the key from over the door and let himself in. Before long, he came out with the shoe on a tray.

The stranger gazed at it. Odd-shaped and nondescript, the shoe appeared to be covered with dull gray pebbles.

"A stone is missing!" he cried out. "Where is the thief?"

Grel swallowed. "It wasn't anyone's fault. You see, there was this beggar girl—"

"The *thief*! Where is he?"

"He was condemned and sent to Mount Xexnax. We may never—"

"Here I am!" Hap Barlo stepped forth from the crowd.

"Hap!" Grel cried. He ran and grabbed the boy in his arms while Rauf barked and jumped as high as his old legs would lift him.

Grel stepped back to get a good look. "Dear boy! You escaped!"

That's when he noticed Silas Barlo the beekeeper standing just to the side and grinning. And next to him, Sophia, who had disappeared so mysteriously a month ago. His eyes blurred with emotion, so that he barely recognized several other long-lost townsmen who'd been sent away long ago. There was even that mischievous lad Markie, who hadn't been seen for years. Here they all were, home again.

"This is a miracle!" he cried. "How—?"

"The stone!" the stranger broke in. "Where is it?"

Hap stopped scratching Rauf's ears and stood up. "I don't have it," he said.

"Ye *steal* it, and then ye *lose* it?" the man fairly roared.

"I am truly sorry," said Hap simply.

"I am sorry, too." There was a pause, like the pause between lightning and thunder. "Are ye sure ye stole it?"

"Oh, very sure."

"Didn't misplace it?"

"Afraid not."

"Maybe put it in the wrong pocket? Have ye checked your pockets?"

"I don't have pockets."

"That is unfortunate. We know about your good qualities."

"You do?"

"Ye almost make the human race bearable."

"I do?"

"But ye leave us no choice."

"I don't?"

The stranger raised his surprisingly short arms and cried, "Execute him, by order of Xexnax!"

The townspeople glanced about, puzzled.

"I see I'll have to do it myself," he said.

"If you have any trouble," boomed another voice, "the Lord Mayor of Aplanap will take care of it!"

For the mayor had just arrived, with Ludmilla the Large at his side, puffing mightily. A contingent of guards began fanning out at the back of the crowd.

The stranger cast a contemptuous eye at the mayor. "Come," he said to Hap, "I need to throw you off the cliff." He seized the boy by the nape of the neck and began dragging him to the precipice.

"Stop!" cried Grel.

"Don't!" begged Silas.

"Rauf!" said Rauf.

"Don't you dare hurt him!" cried Sophia, who had stepped forward and was rotating her outstretched arms in tiny circles. She flung her most fatal curse at the dark stranger.

Nothing happened.

The man turned his baleful eyes upon her. "Ye throw a spell at me?"

"I'll do worse than that!"

"Do not try. Ye are a good human but a very bad magician."

"Then I'll beat you with my fists!" she shouted, and she charged at him full force.

What happened then astonished everyone. When Sophia hurled her skinny shoulder against the stranger, he simply broke in half! The bottom half of him remained standing while the top half toppled backward and landed with a painful thud.

There was a tumult of cloth, and then a strangely hairy head emerged, with heavy brows, sharp blue eyes, and a remarkably long upturned nose.

The townspeople backed away.

"You!" said Hap, who had been thrown free.

"You know this creature?" said the mayor, frowning.

"This is Shadow Reader. He's an Auki."

"So I see."

The bottom half of the stranger thrashed about in the cowl, and then the head of an Auki warrior poked out. Hap recognized him, too. They'd clambered through many tunnels together.

The crowd backed away even farther, although a couple of children had begun to giggle. After all, these Aukis might be fierce-looking, but they weren't very big.

It didn't help that the mayor began laughing as well, and then Ludmilla, whose laugh was louder than anyone's.

"Ye may mock me," declared Shadow Reader, "but ye dare not mock the one I serve."

The mayor tilted back his head to make room for even larger guffaws. "And who do you serve? The queen of the gnomes?"

The laughter had now spread through the crowd. These strange creatures were clearly not to be feared.

"Lord of the leafhoppers?" added the mayor's nephew with a snarky sneer.

"The duke of dung beetles?" cried the mayor, nearly weeping with laughter.

Shadow Reader turned to Hap. "See what ye have done?"

The boy nodded sadly. "All my fault."

"So ye see I really have to execute ye."

"Maybe not," said Hap, backing away. "I can out-run you."

"But you can't," interjected the mayor, stepping forward, "outrun my soldiers. You're surrounded."

It was true. All his men were armed—heavily.

"But why bother them?" said the mayor. He took tight hold of Hap's arm. "I'll do it myself!"

"No!" said Grel.

"Rauf!" said Rauf.

Hap squirmed and twisted but couldn't get free. The mayor had ruled with an iron fist, and now that fist was dragging the boy to the very lip of the cliff. Hap half stumbled, loosening a crumble of dirt that fell, bouncing and spinning, into the void.

"Why," muttered the mayor, "didn't I think of this months ago?"

He braced himself to fling the boy over the edge when his attention was briefly caught by a movement near the front of the crowd. It was a child's hand tugging on the leg of an Auki. The hand belonged to a beggar girl, wound in a filthy green blanket.

"It's her!" said the mayor.

People looked confused.

"Who did he say?"

"Where?"

Shadow Reader felt the tug on his leg and looked down.

The child's hand opened, revealing a gray pebble.

The Auki took it.

"What are you waiting for?" cried Ludmilla the Large, not understanding the delay. "Push!"

The mayor wasn't listening.

Neither was Shadow Reader. He looked at the pebble, then at the one-eyed beggar girl.

Suddenly, he fell to his knees. "Your Majesty!" he cried.

People looked at one another. Several began to giggle.

"Did you hear what he called her?" said one.

"It's that urchin!" Ludmilla exclaimed, squinting at the girl. "The one that started all this!"

The Auki touched his head to the ground. "I have failed you!" he moaned.

The child laid a hand on his scruffy head. For the first time in this whole story, she spoke. Her voice was soft but clear. "You have the stone," she said.

He nodded without raising his head.

"You have a shoemaker."

He nodded again.

"You should be able to think of something."

The Auki raised his head. "You're right, Your Majesty."

He called for Grel.

"Wait!" Ludmilla interrupted. "My husband has to finish pushing that horrible boy off the cliff!"

"In a moment, Luddy dear," said the mayor. He watched as Shadow Reader handed the pebble to Grel, who disappeared inside the shop and returned a minute later with the stone sewn securely in place.

The Auki held it up. Everyone stared. The shoe looked exactly the same.

Almost the same.

Was it possible there was a faint blue cast over it? A shimmer, maybe?

The townspeople crowded closer, the mayor among them. He had forgotten about Hap, who by now had stopped waiting for someone to push him to his death. He easily slid free of the mayor's grasp.

There was no doubt about it; the shoe was glowing.

The blues deepened. The sapphires gleamed. The opals shone. The diamond on the shoe's heel became a fiery star.

"Gimme that thing!" cried Ludmilla, elbowing her way through the crowd.

"Just a moment, madam," said the watchmaker, barring her way.

"You dare stop me?" Ludmilla's eyes flashed.

"I do."

"So do I," said the blacksmith, standing directly in front of her.

"Me too," said the jeweler.

"You!" she cried. "Be warned. I'll take my business elsewhere."

"Oh, thank you!" the jeweler exclaimed. "You haven't paid me for the last seven necklaces."

"*Quiet, everyone!*" called out the beggar girl.

Except for some hard breathing on the part of Ludmilla, the crowd was silent.

"Now," said the girl, letting the green blanket rest comfortably around her shoulders, "bring the thief to me."

The Auki warrior led Hap forward.

"Not him," she said firmly. Small and crippled as she was, her voice held a strange authority. "Three times he saved me. He gave me a fish, a loaf of bread, even a stone from the shoe." She cast her single eye over the crowd. "What he did was wrong, but the stone is back where it belongs now, and I forgive him."

People started whispering. "Did you hear? The beggar forgives him for saving her."

"Such impertinence!"

She pointed her finger at the Lord Mayor of Aplanap. "*That one!*" she declared. "He's the thief."

The mayor shook his head. "Very amusing, I'm sure."

"You deny that you stole cartloads of gems?"

"Stole?"

"Those infernal mines, they belong to you?"

"I don't deny," he replied, "that I run a mining operation on the mountain, if that's what you mean. The stones we harvest are for the general good, and for my fair Ludmilla, who fancies them. I keep nothing for myself, beyond a few bushels of diamonds to cover expenses. What crime have I committed?"

Shadow Reader went up to the mayor and fixed him

with such a deadly stare that the hairs on the man's wart began to shrivel. "Ye have stolen from the goddess, whose mountains these are! Ye have blasted out her treasures and enslaved your fellow humans."

The mayor shrugged. "So?"

The beggar girl directed her single eye at the mayor. "You will put them back."

"I will *what?*"

"You will put the stones back where they came from."

"That's insane! Nobody puts gems *back* in the ground!"

"You will. And your wife will help you."

"Ludmilla?" The mayor snorted. "The fair Ludmilla does not put things back," he said. "She takes things out!"

"Also," the girl continued, "you'll find that your new tasks will take up all your time. Therefore, Hap, the shoemaker's apprentice, will take over as mayor."

The girl's breathtaking audacity extracted a bark of laughter from the mayor, but the laugh died quickly. "All right," he said, "that's enough. Guards! Seize this girl! And see she doesn't get away this time."

The mayor's guards, bristling with weapons, began pushing their way through the crowd.

Things did not look good, it must be said, for Hap and his friends. They had come through many hardships, had even managed a few heroic deeds, but they were weak, small, and unarmed, and the guards were, well, the opposite.

A bull-faced fellow had Sophia by her skinny arm. Another grabbed Hap by his neck. Other guards were getting ready to do violence to Shadow and the beggar girl.

"One moment!" cried the Auki. "Has no one any curiosity about the shoe?"

The crowd began to murmur.

"The shoe," whispered one.

"Oh yes," said another.

"After all," Shadow went on, "it was the shoe that started this trouble."

"True," said the watchmaker's wife.

"Humans," the Auki scoffed. "Ye live on the outside. Always ye go from the outside in, from the top down. Even your religions start with what ye call heaven—"

"What's he gargling about?" griped Ludmilla.

"Enough philosophy," snapped the mayor.

"The goddess," Shadow continued, "rules from the earth up, not from the heavens down."

"Nonsense."

"Instead of a crown, a shoe." Shadow Reader scanned the crowd. "Perhaps it were easier just to show ye." He knelt before the beggar girl. "Is it time, Your Majesty?"

She nodded. "It is more than time. It's going on eternity."

Gently, reverentially, he slipped the gloriously misshapen shoe on the girl's misshapen foot.

A sudden blinding light flashed over the scene. For seconds, no one could see anything. Then the glare began to lessen, and people opened astonished eyes to a vision of the beggar child transforming into a fearsomely beautiful woman, growing taller and taller by the second until her head was nearly out of sight.

At the same moment, all the bells in Aplanap—from the tiniest crystal dinner bell to the church's great gonger—began ringing, binging, and clanging, and flocks of yellow birds exploded into the sky. Cuckoos, they were, thousands of them, freed at last from the prison of their clocks. They cried out in noisy joy, circled the town once, and swept out of sight.

Instinctively, the crowd fell back. Women knelt, men doffed their caps, and Shadow and his fellow Auki stretched prostrate on the ground.

"Xexnax!" Shadow murmured. "Ye have returned."

The vision grew taller yet. It grew upward and downward at once. The blue shoe was no longer a shoe, but the shining waterway known as Doubtful Bay. The goddess's body grew into a mountain range, covered with a green blanket of vegetation. The beggar's one eye glowed as the North Star.

Gradually, the image of the goddess began to fade in the early-evening air, leaving as coordinates the bay; the mountain; the star, glimmering high over the cleansed town.

It took a few moments for the townspeople to notice that the star was floating in a clear sky. The clouds that for so long had covered Aplanap were gone.

"Look!" cried a little child, pulling her mother's dress. "Where did the glass go?"

It was true. The slippery glaze that had covered every roof, road, and streetlamp had simply melted away. The glass-encased beggar by the bank building blinked his eyes and stretched. The quince-picker's goat, which had been the glass statue of a goat, shook its horned head and let out a bleat. Even the glass-coated geraniums in the window boxes were freed of their heavy armor and began to lift their heads.

Hap stood before the townspeople. "It appears," he said, "that I'm to be the new mayor of Aplanap. Is that all right with everybody?"

Whisperings and rumblings scudded through the crowd.

"Fine with me, Hap, my boy!" called out the cheese-maker.

"Isn't he a little young?" objected the baker's wife.

"Thirteen seems a fine age," answered her husband.

"But he's a thief!" called someone else.

"Not half the thief as the mayor!"

"He's a brave lad," called the woodcutter.

Cheers began breaking out. There would have been more, but there in their midst stood the terrifying Ludmilla and her red-faced husband vibrating with rage.

"You'll stop this nonsense right now!" the mayor shouted. *"Guards! Arrest him!"*

The guards hesitated.

Hap threw the men a smile. "Hard to know what to do, isn't it? I understand. But think. You know the kind of mayor you've had. Do you want more of him?"

The guards were not used to thinking for themselves. Their eyes darted back and forth between Hap and the man with the trembling wart.

"You'd better make up your minds," said Hap, "because I'm about to give my first order as the new mayor. Ready? Here it comes: *Guards! Arrest that man!* That woman, too, of course. We wouldn't want to forget the mayor's wife."

"You lay a hand on me," growled Ludmilla, "and I'll have you all ground up for dinner!"

The guards looked at Ludmilla, and then at Hap, and then back at Ludmilla. On one hardened face and then another, the beginnings of a smile appeared, like cracks in stone.

Minutes later, Ludmilla and the mayor—*former* mayor, rather—were marched off to prison to await transport to Mount Xexnax, where they would serve their life sentences. It was agreed that since the human miners were now free, the new prisoners would be guarded by Aukis, who lived in the mountain anyway and would be happy to serve. Naturally, they'd be well paid and provisioned for their work.

"Well," said Grel with a happy sigh, "this calls for schnitzel. Will you join me, Mr. Mayor?"

"Do you have to call me that?"

"You'd better get used to it. And, Miss Sophia, I hope you will join us."

Smiling brightly, Sophia went over and kissed Grel on the cheek.

Twenty-nine

AFTER THE SURPRISES of the past hour, it seemed unlikely there could be another. And yet, when Grel and his friends returned home, they found a long banquet table set out in front, with a linen cloth and scores of covered bowls, platters, and tureens.

Grel blinked. "What's this?"

"I think," said Shadow Reader, "it is best not to question gifts from the goddess."

"But . . . ?"

"No questions." Shadow and the Auki warrior turned to leave.

"Aren't you joining us?"

"Have ye rat-tail soup? Beetle pie? Braised liverwort?"

"I hope not."

"As I thought. In any case, I need to see about my brother."

Hap spoke. "How is Ulf?"

"Mag takes care of him on the ferryboat. I will be helping till he is well."

"So you are friends again?"

"Again? No. For the first time."

Hap gave Shadow a serious look. "Tell me, were you really going to push me off the cliff?"

The old one paused. "I am Auki. I obey."

"What does that mean?" said Hap.

"To bring harm to the shoe is death."

"Death? Really?"

"It is the law. You've seen the shoe. What did ye think it was?"

"Grel's masterpiece. A work of art."

"Don't be so human. Ye saw what happened."

Hap could hardly say *what* he'd seen. "It was amazing."

"It was the goddess. She ordered me to have the shoe made."

"Ordered you?"

"I read her meanings in the shadows."

"But why—?"

"Without the shoe, she could not return."

"I don't understand."

"Ye *would* if ye'd think like an Auki for once. To us, it was never a shoe. It was a door. The door to this world. Her foot was the key."

Hap frowned, trying to take this in. *A door?*

"When the key turned, earth and sky came together, and she was among us again."

"But why," Grel ventured, "would she *want* to be among us, after all those years?"

"The boy can tell ye."

Hap looked at Shadow. "Because of the Great Blue?"

"It's the heart of the heart of the world. To think it almost fell into the hands of humans!"

"I see," said Grel, not really seeing at all. "But why pick me to make the shoe? I'm as human as the rest."

"Look at us." Shadow stood beside his Auki warrior. "Look at our feet."

"Ah."

"We know many things. But not shoes."

Grel smiled. "Glad I could help."

"And you," said Shadow Reader, turning to Hap. "Ye are the leader now. Tell your people to stop taking what does not belong to them." He shook his shaggy head. "The mountain supports us all. We take from it what we need. That is allowed. But enough."

With that, the old Auki turned away. "*More* than enough," he muttered, heading down toward Doubtful Bay.

The friends watched in silence till he was out of sight. Then Grel looked around, dazed by the vast display of food. Neither he nor his dog, Rauf, had eaten a real meal in weeks.

"Speaking of more than enough!" he said. "Sophia, go and tell Jon and your parents to come. And, Hap—I mean, Mayor Barlo—if you think well of it, why not put out the word to any beggars—"

"Done!" Hap set off at a trot.

Twenty minutes later, the long banquet table had a full complement of guests. Rag, the quince-pickers' boy, showed up with his parents, and Jon Hartpence soon arrived with his.

Alas, the elder Hartpences were still bickering, this time about where to sit.

"Sit anywhere!" cried Grel.

"Yes," said Mrs. Hartpence, "but Mr. Hartpence insists on sitting next to the boiled ham, and I must sit where I have a view of the bay."

Sophia shook her head. "I tried," she said.

"What do you mean?" said Jon.

"I kept casting that 'Never-Fail Love Spell' on them."

Hap looked up sharply. "You mean that was for your parents?"

"Who did you think it was for?" Sophia laughed.

Hap blushed furiously.

"You think it was for you, don't you?"

"Of course not!"

"Why would I waste a perfectly good spell on you?" Sophia went on—rather cruelly, it might be said. "I know you already love me!"

This made Mayor Barlo blush even more.

Conversation stopped then as Grel held up his hand. Closing his eyes, he offered thanks to the goddess Xexnax for all the blessings of the earth.

Then Silas stood and sang the song everyone loved, called "The Cuckoos of Aplanap." Several guests found themselves wiping away tears.

Finally, squirming about excitedly, Rauf offered his own blessing—the one word he knew—and the celebration began.

Acknowledgments

Great thanks to Jodi Reamer of Writers House for her excellent representation, to Nancy Siscoe of Knopf for her wise editing, and to both for cheering me on through this book's darkest tunnels.

Roderick Townley has taught in Chile on a Fulbright Fellowship and worked in New York as a journalist. He now writes from his home in Kansas. His highly acclaimed novels include *The Red Thread, Sky,* and the three books of the Sylvie Cycle: *The Great Good Thing, Into the Labyrinth,* and *The Constellation of Sylvie.* In a starred review for *The Great Good Thing, Kirkus Reviews* raved, "Townley has created that most impossible thing: a book beloved from the first page."

You can read more about Roderick Townley and his books at rodericktownley.com.

Mary GrandPré is perhaps best known for creating the jackets and illustrations for the Harry Potter books. She has also illustrated many fine picture books, including *Chin Yu Min and the Ginger Cat* by Jennifer Armstrong and *Lucia and the Light* by Phyllis Root. You can read more about Mary GrandPré and her work at marygrandpre.com.